THE

MISSING

TWO

First edition published in 2024
© Copyright 2024
Allison Osborne

The right of Allison Osborne to be identified as the author of this work has been asserted by him in accordance with the Copyright, Designs and Patents Act 1998.
All rights reserved. No reproduction, copy or transmission of this publication may be made without express prior written permission. No paragraph of this publication may be reproduced, copied or transmitted except with express prior written permission or in accordance with the provisions of the Copyright Act 1956 (as amended). Any person who commits any unauthorised act in relation to this publication may be liable to criminal prosecution and civil claims for damage.

All characters appearing in this work are fictitious. Any resemblance to real persons, living or dead, is purely coincidental. The opinions expressed herein are those of the author and not of Orange Pip Books.

Paperback ISBN: 978-1-80424-446-3
ePub ISBN: 978-1-80424-447-0
PDF ISBN: 978-1-80424-448-7

Published by Orange Pip Books
335 Princess Park Manor, Royal Drive,
London, N11 3GX
www.orangepipbooks.com

HOLMES & CO. MYSTERIES

COLLECTION ONE
THE INTRODUCTION OF HOLMES & CO
A STUDY IN VICTORY RED
THE CIRCLE CODE CONUNDRUM
THE IMPOSSIBLE MURDERER
THE HAPPY FAMILY FACADE
THE RED ROVER SOCIETY
THE DETECTIVE'S NEMESIS

COLLECTION TWO
THE ADVENTURES OF HOLMES & CO.
THE HIDDEN CASE
THE MISSING TWO
THE AMERICAN VISITORS

Try to realize what we do know so as to make the most of it, and to separate the essential from the accidental.

-Sherlock Holmes, *The Adventure of the Priory School*

Chapter I

A Curiously Vague Request

221 Baker Street's small back garden was in serious need of repair. Clad in jackets and wellies, Irene Holmes and Doctor Joe Watson surveyed that morning's work.

The pair had promised Miss Hudson a vegetable garden in the far corner with a flower bed on the opposite side. But the lot had sprouted weeds the size of footballs and half the ground was still squishy. Despite the hours of labour already behind them, there was still much to be done.

Joe had taken a few days off to help with the garden, which had been a sweet gesture admittedly, given that he much preferred to vaccinate canines and inspect felines for ticks. Especially since now, he struggled over a piece of debris from the fallen building next door.

Meanwhile, Isla the West Highland Terrier – now a rousing eight months old and a holy terror in her own right – had found a dozen things of interest amongst the underbrush. Dirt and God knew what else smeared her rough white fur. She'd also chased, and almost caught, several mice so far.

As much as she was distracting, Isla kept Irene lighthearted as the day dragged on. Physical labour was abhorring as ever; Irene desperately clung to the hope that she would find something buried in the dirt.

"There aren't even any interesting *plants*!"

From beside her, Joe leaned on his rake, cheeks red. "What kinds were you hoping for?"

"Oh, I don't know. Any poisonous plant would do, but there are none!"

"I shouldn't have to say this out loud, but," Joe paused for emphasis, "please do not grow poisonous plants in Miss Hudson's garden."

Irene playfully scoffed, shoving a rogue curl of hair away. "I will not. Mostly because I don't want her to mix some up in our salads. Now, let's get a move on before I leave the work to you entirely."

Almost an hour later, her patience was so thin it was practically transparent. She yanked at a particularly large weed with all her strength, cuss words flying across her mind.

All the while Joe looked at her, but not quizzically. No, it was more wary, hesitant. Since they'd started back up, something clearly plagued his thoughts, but he made no attempts to voice it, rather looking downward instead. Whatever he wanted to ask required courage. Which meant it was rather intrusive, as their friendship had long surpassed awkward topics.

It was either about her father or about his progressing relationship with Sarah, the librarian, with whom he was getting increasingly more serious.

Joe turned over the soil once more.

Irene rolled her eyes, gave one final tug, and the weed popped out of the ground. She stood with it still in her fist, and turned to her friend.

"What is it you want to ask me?"

"I don't know what—"

"My dear Joe." Dirt flew as she put her hand on her hip. "You may mask all your emotions and thoughts out in public, but you are an open book at Baker Street. And this weeding is quite tedious. So, please, do interrupt with something hopefully of value."

Joe poked the ground with the rake. "I was just… Please tell me if I am overstepping—"

"I always do, though you rarely overstep. Pray, continue."

He refused to meet her eyes.

So, it had to do with Sherlock Holmes.

"I was thinking about your father…" Joe started, gaze flashing to hers for a brief second. "Do you know how his bees fared during the winter? I know you don't talk to Miss Hudson about him much, and you have yet to write that letter. Nevertheless, I was curious…."

Surprisingly, her ribs didn't tighten and no lump clumped in her throat.

Irene was better now at dealing with her complicated emotions regarding her father, especially since she'd discovered that Miss Hudson visited him at least once a month and that his nurse was of decent skill.

The thoughts still made her palms itch, however, and she'd taken to chewing the inside of her bottom lip. To distract herself, she looked at the weed she'd plucked moments before.

"To be honest with you, I have been thinking of them myself. I considered asking Miss Hudson, but never worked up the courage to do so. You may ask, if you wish."

She kept her eyes down.

Irene knew her friend had countless questions about her father and Uncle John. The more Joe read his stories, the more quizzical he became. A part of her wished to blurt out the entire story and every feeling that came with it, but even entertaining that idea churned her insides. So, Joe received little bits of information whenever her body didn't revolt at the thought of speaking them.

"But you've been doing so well, I would hate to have you revert—"

"You may ask," Irene snapped. She softened her voice, remembering that this was her best friend, not some stranger on the street. "Then relay the answer to me, if you would."

Joe gave her shoulder a small squeeze. "Of course."

The back door burst open and Miss Hudson hurried out.

The pair whirled around in synchronisation. Joe held his rake out like a sword, ready to thrash at an attacker. Irene raised her fists in a boxing stance, weed still between her fingers.

"Heavens, it's only me! Don't attack!"

"Goodness' sake, Miss Hudson, has someone caught on fire?!" Irene flung the weed to the ground.

The older woman's eyes widened, her white hair puffed up. "Why is that the first scenario to pop into your head?"

"Because I would expect that kind of reaction. But here you are, holding an envelope." She plucked the paper.

Miss Hudson scoffed and slapped her hands. "Irene Holmes! Just because you are tired, dirty, and grumpy, does *not* mean you can snatch things from me."

Her Scottish brogue thickened with every word, causing Irene to shrink back a little, her inner chastised child emerging.

"I apologise, Miss Hudson."

Joe clasped a hand over his upturned mouth.

The landlady caught wind of him, however, and rounded on the poor man. He straightened, not daring to upset her again.

She pointed at the envelope that had fallen in the dirt. "That is from Madame Joffrey's School for Charming Young Women, sealed with wax and everything."

"A finishing school? I thought the frivolity of those went out with the war?"

"Oh, heavens no. Etiquette is always important."

"And that's why you rushed out here?" Irene raised a brow. "Wait! Miss Hudson, you didn't sign *me* up, did you?"

The woman let out a great bark of laughter. "Goodness no. This is a small but *very* prestigious school. I assume they want your help with something. It's nice to see your reputation circling amongst the elite. Heaven knows that your father's name was everywhere foul places and all. Names like these will keep *you* amongst the privileged, in good health, safe, and home. Now, you two go wash up—"

Irene ripped at the blue wax seal, smearing dirt all over the crisp stationery. Noting the pounds stuffed inside, she handed the envelope to Joe, who prepared to read over her shoulder.

The stationery was thick and expensive, with an emblem embellished into the corner. Though the handwriting was pretty and flowing, there was a slight shakiness to it:

Miss Holmes,

Come at once. Your assistance is required for a sensitive matter. Travelling funds enclosed within.

Miss Flaversham

"Nothing as to *why*, or what tools to bring, or anything at all!"

Joe shrugged. "Perhaps it's a very important matter that requires being discreet. A school full of young women would draw attention should anything go wrong."

"I suppose," Irene huffed. "But we don't know if this is a stolen object, a missing person, a murder, or someone just forgot to curtsy while balancing a teacup on their head."

"I don't think they teach that."

Irene answered Joe's raised brow with her own. She faced Miss Hudson again. "Write to them and tell them we are on the way. Give them a list of our fees and recommendations for suitable accommodations."

Miss Hudson nodded. "As much as I love you solving these mysteries, I do sometimes wish you had a proper secretary."

Irene waved the woman off, mind already working. "All in good time."

Isla scurried past them then as if sensing the mystery afoot.

Miss Hudson cried out. "Good heavens! This dog smells like worms!"

"An actual case, Joe," Irene turned to her partner, ignoring the stricken woman's woes. "*Hopefully*. The last one was too convoluted. Now, this is how it's supposed to be done – someone seeks out our services and we jump in with both feet."

He followed her to the back door. "If they make you balance a teacup on your head, may I take a picture?"

"Perhaps."

"Away we go, then!"

* * * * *

Madame Joffrey's School for Charming Young Women sat in a small valley off the main road on the outskirts of Surrey. Irene and Joe arrived by mid-afternoon with plenty of daylight left for whatever mystery the school held.

Irene drove their '37 Vauxhall into the small car park. The facility itself was unassuming. It had three neat, flat buildings attached to one another in a U shape, all untouched from the war. The front gardens were immaculate, even for this time of year, which made Irene think of all the weeds in her own backyard. A hedge on the verge of greening surrounded the smooth red brick. The school was in a secluded area, separated from farms outside the town by a field which, in turn, lead into a forest.

A young woman greeted them at the double front door, taking their overnight bags for storage. Another one, with a dress freshly pressed, took over as they went inside. She gave them a quick look, then attempted to hide her shy smile as she led them down the hallway.

Irene looked at her own clothes, then at Joe's, and almost snorted. They had once again unintentionally matched outfits. He wore brown trousers with a matching vest over a white shirt, while she sported tan trousers and a white blouse. Her hat was the same tweed as his vest.

The young lady led them through a long hallway lined with pictures of graduating classes over the years. A large portrait of a stern-looking elderly woman hung in the middle; the label read *Madame Joffrey*.

"You're going to meet with Miss Flaversham today."

"She took over from Madame Joffrey?" Joe asked.

"Correct."

"I will admit," Irene said as they approached an office door. "I didn't know Madames held titles at finishing schools."

"Where else would they work?"

"The Madame I know runs a brothel."

The woman's cheeks flushed, but she said nothing.

She gave a quick knock. A sharp command to enter sounded from the other side.

Everything about the room was as neat as it went. The walls were lined with bookcases, boasting large volumes. The desk in the centre smelled of freshly polished wood. Everything was impeccably organised – not one pencil or paper out of place.

Miss Flaversham was the embodiment of grace and perfection. She was in her mid-forties, hair fashioned in a bun, nails short and glossy, and her dress was impeccably ironed.

The elegant woman seemed to glide as she went around the desk, ready to greet the pair. She stretched out her hand.

Overtaken by the pristine environment, Joe gave the most awkward bow instead. Thankfully, their host had good spirits – inclining her head slightly, she reciprocated with a delicate curtsy.

"It is very nice to meet you, Doctor. And you must be Miss Holmes. Your trousers are very becoming."

"Thank you." Irene stuck out her hand and was met with a firm grip. "Your note was brief and hurried, everything appears calm here."

The headmistress gestured for all to sit. "The incident is cause for much concern, but running around in hysterics is not in our etiquette. Allow me to explain."

Irene bit her lip to keep from smiling as Joe sat pin-straight, shoulders square and attentive, as if trying to impress. Her own posture was always quite good, unless she was pondering.

As if sensing her thoughts, Miss Flaversham gave her a small nod of approval. Irene resisted the urge to roll her eyes. They weren't here for a lesson in etiquette; they were here to solve a mystery.

"Last night, two of our eldest girls went missing," Miss Flaversham started. "We believe they left on their own accord as opposed to a kidnapping."

"What is the reason for this belief?" Irene asked.

"No windows were broken; the rooms were neat. Not one girl heard screams or cries in the middle of the night either."

"Tell me about them."

Accustomed to the process, Joe already had his notebook out.

"One of the girls, Charlotte Bancroft, is a top student. She seemed to enjoy all the lessons. Her family is exceptionally well off, if I may say so." Flaversham paused and dipped her head, whispering. "Everything discussed will be kept discreet and private, right, Miss Holmes?"

"Of course." Irene answered immediately. "Doctor Watson keeps a record of the case, but it is for our eyes only."

The woman gave a curt nod, then continued. "There were rumours that a gentleman would come calling on Charlotte, but I saw nothing of the sort."

She adjusted some papers on her desk. Irene couldn't tell if she was lying or if she was simply nervous. Men had easy tells;

they were as transparent as a washed window most of the time. But women were slightly trickier to decode.

Joe spoke, "How well do the groundskeepers know the students?"

"Not well at all. We only have them here on weekends – when the girls are either away to visit home, or are otherwise preoccupied. Lord knows that there are enough distractions at their age. I did question both groundskeepers, but Mr. Tulley was at home with his wife last night, and the other admitted to being at the pub. If I may be so bold, he smelled of it too."

"Solid alibis for them both," Irene regarded the headmistress. "Well done."

Miss Flaversham had managed to impress her. Though Irene didn't agree with her occupation and overall institution, the woman was quite intelligent and proactive. "Have any of the girls offered information?"

"None have come forward, but I will give you a list of who to question."

"Excellent. Now, tell us about the other missing girl."

The headmistress adjusted her nameplate. Her lips were pursed, hiding annoyance and frustration.

After a brief moment, she seemed to collect herself. "I dislike speaking ill of my students. I believe every young woman has the capability to become a well-mannered lady. But Lizzie Roberts is different. Though she did well in her studies, it was clear she had another life in mind. She has always been desperate to leave the school. I wouldn't be surprised if she ran away for the sake of dramatics. But she is a student here, and her disappearance needs to be remedied before it tarnishes the school's reputation."

"How well did she know Charlotte?"

"They were acquaintances at best. I don't expect all my students to become the best of friends, but there is a certain level of respect and decorum that I demand. That being said, they did not engage in the same social circles."

"Have you talked to Scotland Yard at all?"

"I have not. I was hoping to solve this quickly without much fanfare. I have no desire to contact the police, nor alert the girls' families."

Joe shifted in his seat. "May I ask why? Perhaps they went home. If not, their family members could provide insight as to their whereabouts. Not to mention that Scotland Yard certainly has more resources to trace missing persons better than us."

Irene watched the woman adjust the papers again and the wheels in her head spun faster. "Because Scotland Yard would be obligated to contact the families – who are all well off, I'll dare to assume – and they may go public with the news. A scathing article wouldn't do the school any good, would it?"

"I am not proud of the secrecy, but I cannot let this school fail. It did not survive the horrors of the war to be brought down with one silly scandal."

"What about the girls' rooms? I will investigate them, of course, but did you see anything out of the ordinary upon first inspection?"

"Nothing of note. Charlotte's bed was made, with everything in order. Lizzie's bed was unmade, but she always kept her room relatively neat."

"Very good. May we speak to the other girls now?"

"Of course."

Miss Flaversham stood and led them out. They passed a mathematics classroom and another with rows of expensive sewing machines, projects hanging all over the desks.

Joe spoke as they continued down the halls. "I will admit, I am impressed by your facility. Not that I've given much thought to a woman's finishing school, or what it would entail, but the classrooms are very intriguing."

Their host chuckled lightly. "Thank you, Doctor. We strive to teach more than how to balance a teacup and saucer on our heads."

At that, Joe raised his brow at Irene. In turn, she responded with an eye roll. Although, she was just as impressed with the school. Perhaps the facility could have benefited from a self-defence or weapons class, but she was not as disgusted as she anticipated.

Chatter from at least a dozen young women reached their ears as they approached a large hall. Irene braced herself. This would either go extremely well or the next hour would descend into chaos. Either the girls would immediately find opportunities to gossip and let out all their own grievances with either the school or the missing girls; Or they'd take to swooning at Joe and his windswept ginger hair and tall stature.

Chapter II

Madame Joffery's School for Charming Young Women

Questioning the young women was both easier and stranger than Joe expected. Most of them simply giggled or gave half-answers with varying details, but they all seemed to want to take part.

Irene asked Miss Flaversham to wait in her office since the students would likely answer more truthfully without her presence. So far, that hypothesis proved to be correct.

There was, in fact, a young man who came to visit Charlotte Bancroft frequently, but the description of him differed from statement to statement. Joe scribbled down each descriptor in case they could make sense of it later.

It was now down to the last two girls. One looked extremely bored, and the other – whose name was Annette –wouldn't take her eyes off Irene, blushing and giggling like the others had at

Joe.

Annette proved to be the most helpful so far as she knew both missing young women.

"Charlotte had a boy come round," she said. Her back was straight, with hands delicately placed in her lap, and her gaze never wavered from Irene. "I saw him several times. His hair was dark and to his shoulders. I couldn't tell you his height, but if you found a footprint, you could tell from that, right?"

Irene nodded. "The ground is soft, though. An imprint may stay or simply be washed away."

"Oh." Annette furrowed her brow. "You're right. I was trying to gather all the clues for you, I'm sorry that I fell short. I think it's brilliant what you do. My dream is to be a detective one day."

"There is nothing stopping you."

The girl looked rueful now. "My family would simply not have it if I quit school to chase criminals. And Scotland Yard will not make me a DI."

Joe addressed the student's infatuation with the oblivious Irene with a smile. Miss Hudson's earlier comment about the need for a secretary surfaced in his mind. If any woman would want that job, it would be Annette.

Of course, they'd have to have an actual office, which meant having a legitimate business, and a different telephone number…

"Those are all good observations," Irene said, bumping him gently with her elbow. "What have you observed about Lizzie?"

The young woman beside Annette chimed in for the first time. "She was one of my best mates, but even I didn't know she was going to run away."

Joe scribbled down notes. "You think she ran away? Not collected by some boy?"

"She hated it here. My guess is that she saw Charlotte leaving with her boyfriend and took off as well."

"One more question before we let you return to your studies," Irene said. "Would Miss Flaversham have known about this boy who visited Charlotte? Would she have chased him away at all?"

They both nodded.

"She has," Annette said. "More than a few times."

The pair exchanged curious looks. The headmistress had neglected to give them this information. In fact, if Joe recalled correctly, she never mentioned knowing at all. He was slightly disappointed that she hadn't been as forthcoming as she'd appeared. They had to retrace their steps, more aggressively this time. Beside him, Irene was already balling her fist and pursing her lips, eager to confront Miss Flaversham.

"I believe that's all we need from you both," he hurried to wrap up the conversation before his partner simply left. "Thank you for the time. You've both been very helpful."

The other girl made a quick getaway then, but Annette stuck to

Irene like a lost puppy.

"Have we? I do hope so! And if you need anything more, Miss Holmes, I'm sure Miss Flaversham will let me speak with you."

Irene paused and regarded the young woman, but instead of berating or dismissing her, she spoke directly and friendly. "If you are so eager, you may keep your eyes open for anything new or suspicious. Do *not* involve yourself or interfere. Write us a letter or ring us on the telephone if it is urgent."

She flicked her hand at Joe, and he dug out their business card. The girl took it, eyes sparkling.

"Oh, yes, Miss Holmes. I will, indeed! Thank you!"

Irene stiffened, anticipating a hug, but Annette surprised her by sticking out her hand. They shook once before the girl flitted out of the room.

"I like her. She would make a fine secretary, you know. Should we ever have an office, that is."

"I was thinking the same thing," Joe said.

"Sometimes your intelligence climbs up to my level."

"I like to think I stay there for a short while at least."

"Occasionally," Irene teased. Then suddenly, her eyebrows drew inward. "All those women had different descriptions of the boy that visited Charlotte. Long hair. Cropped hair. Tall, short, long legs, dark eyes. The more we asked, the more they started describing *you*, for heaven's sake!"

"At least we know there was, in fact, a boy."

"And that Miss Flaversham has some explaining to do." She marched down the hall.

Joe jogged to catch up to her.

"Keep your head, Irene. There must be a good reason she didn't give us this information. The woman has been more than forthcoming with everything else."

The sleuth didn't slow her step, but her shoulders relaxed. "I have a feeling it has to do with money. It *always* has to do with money. The richer you are, the more secrecy you're allowed."

Once they reached the office, Irene opened the door without waiting for an invitation. Miss Flaversham stood immediately as if she were expecting them.

Irene folded her arms across her chest. "You've kept information from us."

Joe stepped between them, always prepared to diffuse the situation. "Miss Flaversham, forgive us for barging in. New information has come to light about the boy that visited Charlotte."

"Apparently there's been many witnesses," Irene interjected. "I find it hard to believe you have not at least heard some of these descriptions, or even seen the boy yourself."

The woman sighed. "I was trying to be discreet. I thought if we could avoid contacting any outside family, that would be ideal."

"There are children missing! This is no time to be *discreet*."

"They are not children, Miss Holmes."

"Yes, they are. That is why two of them are missing. An unfinished brain breeds spontaneity. Now tell us all about this boy that visits."

The headmistress settled back into her seat, sighing.

Irene, however, remained upright.

Joe put his hand on her shoulder, squeezing ever so slightly. He felt her relax under his touch and take a deep breath as they both sat across from the headmistress once again.

"I've only chased him away twice. His name is Tobias Clarke III," Miss Flaversham's tone deepened at the boy's frivolous title.

"And his address?"

Silence.

"Miss Flaversham, either you give us the address, or we find it ourselves. But to do that, we have to tell people why. All of your attempts to keep this charade a secret will be out the window."

The headmistress stared at the determined detective across from her for a solid thirty seconds before pursing her lips.

"While I do not like the threat, I see your point. I shall write it down for you. But, please, as a favour to me, be discreet."

Joe tucked the piece of stationery into his notebook once Miss Flaversham had finished noting the boy's address.

"He is no stranger to the school. His family and the Bancrofts are intertwined. But Charlotte hardly seems the type to run off with him. She is intelligent, with such a bright future. And he is... Well, Tobias is a rich boy who evaded the war and now runs around spending his parents' money."

"All the more reason for us to investigate him. I'll also be honest with you. We will eventually have to inform Charlotte's parents. We cannot keep them in the dark. And they may provide useful information."

"I am aware, Miss Holmes." Flaversham sighed. "I simply don't need a panic at this moment."

"We'll attempt to keep panic at a minimum." Irene stood. "Now, show us the girls' rooms."

* * * * *

Each young woman had their own room that housed a bed, night table, a small dresser and standing mirror. The accommodations quarter was located at the back of the building where the field met the forest, with a clear view of anyone trying to sneak up on the school.

Joe stood at the door of Charlotte's room, taking in the bigger picture. Irene, per usual, was on her hands and feet, stomach almost flat on the ground like a lizard. Miss Flaversham made a small, startled grunting noise as she watched Irene scuttle about.

"Perhaps I shall leave you to your investigation? There is much I have to attend to—"

"I would prefer it. Fewer faces looming over me while I work."

Joe attempted to make up for Irene's lack of manners. "Her direct answers must account for some form of etiquette?"

The woman shook her head, then left the room.

The good doctor did his duty, looking at the furniture, but saw not one item out of place. Everything was dusted and polished.

A collection of perfumes sat atop the dresser. The number stood out to him. While some women liked to collect scents, most had one or two that they preferred. He inspected the bottles, poking at some. Upon his movement, Irene popped up beside him.

"Curious. So many."

She spritzed one of the fuller ones on her wrist. A pleasant citrus and rose scent with a hint of a deeper, musky smell dispersed throughout the room.

"That smells rather nice," Joe remarked.

"It does." Irene sniffed her wrist again.

"It's *Ma Griffe, Carven*. From France." A chipper voice came from the doorway.

Both turned to find Annette at the door, beaming.

"Charlotte has so many that she usually gives most of them away. She has an affinity for impulse purchases or she receives them as gifts. Like that one – her father brought it back from a trip. She doesn't like the lemon scent, though."

Joe glanced at the perfume again. "Perhaps when the investigation is over, we…"

He watched as Irene shoved the bottle into her bag before turning back to her search.

Annette giggled, then saw Joe's worried expression. "Oh, it's okay, Doctor. She won't even realise it's missing."

"That's not the point…"

Joe attempted once more to glean anything from the pristine room, but found nothing. Charlotte had left the space in tiptop shape before vanishing.

"It's curious her bed was made. Obviously she did it before she stole away into the night."

Irene nodded but didn't comment. She simply stared at the window. Even closed, there was a slight draft coming through. His friend tilted her head like a dog, then took to the floor again, scurrying toward the bed. Reaching under, she snatched something.

"Ah ha!" she said, coming up with a piece of paper in her hand. "School stationary. A little dusty, but recently fallen."

It turned out to be a letter to the headmistress:

Dear Miss Flaversham,

As you have noticed, I am gone. Many apologies if I have caused a panic. But don't worry, as I have merely travelled up to my family's cottage on the north shore. My mother and father know all about this plan, so no need to bother them with any fuss. I shall return promptly, but not sooner than a fortnight.

All the best.

Charlotte

As if summoned by the writing, Miss Flaversham reappeared at the doorway.

Joe read the letter to her, then tucked it into his notebook. "Has she mentioned this home before?"

"No. But I wouldn't be surprised if the Bancroft's own several properties along the coast. What do you make of it, Miss—"

Her eyes widened. Joe turned to see the cause of her shock.

Irene was leaning out of the now fully open window. She hoisted a leg up, then disappeared over the windowsill.

Miss Flaversham gasped. But Joe – used his partner's antics – simply strolled over.

She landed easily enough and poked around the grass. Pointing back up, she addressed Joe, "Grass flattened. No footprints as there's been too much activity."

"Miss Holmes!" The headmistress hurried over. "What do you think of this letter?"

Irene waved her off, not even looking up. "Inconsequential."

"In what manner?"

The sleuth popped up between Joe and Miss Flaversham, calling Annette into the room. "Has Charlotte mentioned this house in any capacity before?"

"Not at all, Miss Holmes."

"And yet this boy she's spoken about several times."

"Yes."

Irene twirled her wrist as if that gave the woman the answer she sought. She then held her hand out to Joe and used his strength to hoist herself up.

Once in the room again, Irene clasped her hands together. "On to Lizzie's, if you please."

* * * * *

Lizzie's room provided even fewer clues. Her bed was unmade; there were some stockings and a pair of shoes left on the floor. Her closet was empty.

There were no signs of a forced entry.

Irene held her hand at the windowsill, then gestured to the frame.

Joe picked up on her instruction, but the window wouldn't budge. He tried to jiggle the pane, but to no avail.

"Some of them are stiff," Miss Flaversham offered.

Annette piped up from behind the headmistress. "Lizzie's window never really worked."

Irene paced in the small space. "She would've had to leave through Charlotte's window, if they snuck out together."

As Joe was about to sort some of his own ideas out, his partner clapped her hands. "We shall be off now."

"Already, Miss Holmes? Have you solved anything?"

"Lots. But not enough. We will most likely be back with further questions. For now, hire some security to keep watch should the girls return. I doubt they will, but one never knows with teenagers. In saying that, should you find out any more information, please contact us immediately. We have stops to make on our way back, but are staying at the lovely hotel just inside town that you recommended. Good day."

She strode out of the room, leaving both the headmistress and Annette staring after her.

* * * * *

The large, rectangular Clarke residence sat at the bottom of a hill. It looked pristine from afar, but as they pulled into the gravel laneway, Joe noticed everything could use a touch-up. The pair exited the car and he studied the bushes around the front door.

"Is it me or could these use a watering?"

Irene agreed, kicking at the stones beneath her. "This also needs a raking. And I'll bet a cookbook of Miss Hudson's recipes that round the sides and back of the house haven't been touched in a long while either."

He rapped on the door. It took a long minute for a worn-out housekeeper to greet them.

"Good afternoon," Joe began. "We're here to speak with Mr. and Mrs. Clarke."

If the woman was worried or suspicious, she did not show. Following behind her, Joe and Irene entered a sitting room with just enough furniture to fill the space. He got the feeling that most possessions had been sold.

"Do you get the impression that they cannot afford such a house?"

Irene nodded. "I noticed that immediately. Lack of nice furniture and one maid who looks run off her feet."

"Keeping up appearances is tough."

"Especially when others think you still have money."

Mr. and Mrs. Clarke entered the room as if they were in the company of the Queen, gliding across the carpet and sitting next to one another on the sofa. They both wore evening wear more suited for a fancy event.

Joe waited for Irene to speak. She gave the older couple a quick once-over, then plastered a fake smile on her face.

"Your son, Tobias. Is he here?"

Mr. Clarke shook his head, bulldog jowls jiggling. "He left yesterday."

"That's what I suspected. I will be frank with you. He has been seen frequenting Madame Joffrey's Finishing School where one of the girls, Charlotte Bancroft, has gone missing. We have reason to believe she has run off with him, or rather, Tobias has taken her away."

The Clarkes regarded the detective for the briefest of seconds, but their faces remained neutral. Joe found the whole interaction very odd and scribbled notes to discuss afterwards.

Irene crossed her arms. "You don't appear concerned that you son has potentially run away with a young woman."

Mrs. Clarke shrugged her bony shoulders. "They've known each other since infancy. They were set to be wed once she became of age."

"They were engaged?" Joe asked.

"Not officially, but we'd planned their pairing from the beginning – our house and theirs. Perhaps they've eloped."

"And would her parents approve of this elopement?"

"I'm sure they will, when they realise what a fine young man our Tobias has become."

"So, you are not concerned at all?" Joe scribbled a bunch of question marks in his notebook.

The woman gave another shrug. "I would liked to be at the wedding, but I'm sure he will return with his bride once they've had their fun."

Her nonchalant attitude settled in his stomach like a too-greasy full English. He knew that many families were more lenient with their sons compared to their daughters, but the Clarkes didn't appear to have any qualms about Tobias taking Charlotte away to marry her.

Irene huffed, also ruffled by their nonchalance. "Well, there are many people concerned about the girl, so if they do return, please let us know lest we ring Scotland Yard and report a kidnapping."

This statement caught Mrs. Clarke's attention who sat a bit straighter. "My son didn't kidnap anyone!"

The sleuth stood and motioned for Joe to do the same. "If he returns home, contact us and have him prove it. Because, right now, there is a missing girl and all hypotheses point to this conclusion."

With those final words, Irene marched out the door. Joe closed his notebook and strode after her into the cool evening.

* * * * *

"Do you think he truly kidnapped her?" He asked as Irene pulled on to the main road toward town.

She chewed her lip. "No. Her handwriting was hurried but not shaky. But if she had eloped with the person she was meant to marry anyway, why not state that? Why make up a story about a house on the coast?"

"So, she has run away. But why? By the headmistress's words, Charlotte was doing well and seemed happy at the school."

"Just because someone is doing well does not mean they are happy."

Joe sighed. "This is true. Tobias' parents appeared almost gleeful at the idea he'd stolen her away."

"It is curious. Let's hope they actually contact us if they hear anything. It is time to talk to Charlotte's parents, though. They might provide insight. Perhaps she'd contacted them this whole time and we will wrap up this mystery tonight."

"Charlotte's, at least. We have Lizzie's disappearance to solve as well."

"All in good time. She simply ran is what I suspect. No hiding, no tricks. She didn't like where she was, so she left. Now, on to the Bancroft estate."

Joe checked his watch. "It is late, Irene. Do we bother them at his hour? Especially given what Miss Flaversham said about wanting to keep this whole affair quiet?"

"Yes," she said, turning down a laneway to another affluent road. "If only to catch them off guard. But we will be brief. If they have any knowledge of their daughter's whereabouts, I want to know immediately."

Chapter III
The Bancroft Estate

Joe let out a low whistle. The house they pulled into was a small castle, with property that stretched out into the night. Irene too had to admit that she was impressed by the stature of the estate. Even in the dim light, the grounds were immaculate; the drive was well-swept and groomed. Judging by the light shining inside several second-story balconies, they belonged to one room – most likely a spacious bedroom.

"Do you think *their* rooms are full of furniture?" Joe asked as they stepped up the wide stairs to the large double door.

"I believe even their closets have furniture."

Irene gave a sharp knock on the door. Within a minute, a bright-eyed butler answered. "Name and business?"

"Irene Holmes and my colleague, Dr. Watson. We're private investigators here to ask Mr. and Mrs. Bancroft some questions."

The man simply stared at them.

She sighed. "A card, if you please, Doctor."

Digging into his notebook, he handed a card to her, and she held it out for the butler.

"Step inside."

They entered into a grand foyer that towered about them, giving way to a large, intricate chandelier.

The man led them into a sitting room that could've doubled as a ballroom, every inch set with rich fabrics and luxurious furniture that had to be from last century.

"Wait here a moment."

Irene and Joe took up a seat on an overstuffed couch. She bit back a chuckle as the doctor stroked the fine finishings.

"This place is ridiculous. We could fit everyone we know with room to spare!" his eyes were wide as dinner plates.

"Everyone?" Irene asked, amused at his wonder.

"Me, you, Miss Hudson, my sisters, my parents, your father, Lestrade, and DI Gregory, if he were so inclined, and I don't think we'd even see each other."

"And who would get the enormous bedroom with its own balcony?"

He blew a quiet raspberry. "Oh hell, it's big enough that you and I could share it and still have to shout at each other across the room."

Irene couldn't help smiling as she pictured herself and

everyone she knew waltzing about this massive estate. Joe's exclusion of Sarah was curious, however, whether it was on purpose or not. Instead of asking about it, though, she thought of another subject of conversation. She felt proud for recognising that pestering him about Sarah would have been intrusive and inappropriate at this particular time.

"Why do you want a house so big, anyway? Baker Street seems plenty enough for us."

"Oh, Baker Street is wonderful. You know how much I love it there. But a place like this has a certain security in knowing that your family always has somewhere to stay. And that you have the means to take care of anyone else who should be in need of help."

The butler interrupted their conversation as he ushered in the second pair of completely done-up individuals for the night. Though, the Bancrofts appeared to have the means and wares to do so with conviction.

Irene picked out the slight shift in the woman's fabric, and the man's socks – one blue and the other black. Both indicators of a rushed affair. She almost rolled her eyes at the fact that they put on their finest simply to meet two private investigators.

They stood to greet the distinguished couple.

"Mr. and Mrs. Bancroft," Joe held out his hand. "Thank you for seeing us. We have a few questions, then we will let you retire for the evening."

Mr. Bancroft gestured for one of them to start speaking as he lit a cigarette. Meanwhile, Mrs. Bancroft pulled out a long, red holder and lit her own.

"My first question," Irene began, "is about your house on the north coast. Is it still functional?"

Mr. Bancroft leaned forward, bushy eyebrows drawing together.

"Now, why are you asking about that?"

"Your daughter Charlotte mentioned visiting it, and I was curious."

"We sold it just before the war," he said, brows still tight. "Whatever state it's in belongs to the new owners."

"So, there is no reason for your daughter, Charlotte, to stay in it?"

"She's only ever been there once. And she hated it. I doubt she'd even remember where it was as she was very young. What is this about?"

"We received a call from Madame Joffrey's Finishing School stating that Charlotte had run away. She left a note saying that she was going to your house on the coast."

The man was on his feet in an instant. "What? Why weren't we contacted?"

Irene stood to match him, crossing her arms. "We are here now in the thick of the investigation. She does not appear to be in any danger. Rest assured that we will find her. There is possible evidence she may have left with Tobias Clarke. Can you add anything to this narrative?"

Mr. Bancroft huffed at her, chest heaving. His wife clutched a handkerchief to her face.

"She hasn't spoken to him in years, I thought."

Now that he was calming down, they both sat again.

The man looked at his wife. "Do you know anything?"

The woman dabbed her eyes. "They were supposed to be wed, but their family fell on such hard times that we were under the assumption they had called it off. We haven't even heard from them for close to a year now. Charlotte always said he was brash and rude. She's never liked him."

"The Clarkes are under the impression that they are still promised to each other."

"Given their finances and my daughter's opinion of him, we were considering other options for her. You really think she's run off with him?"

"You would be a better judge of her character than us. If you believe she hasn't, then this changes the case slightly."

Mr. Bancroft shifted, ready to stand again. "You should've come straight to us instead of the Clarkes. Of course they wouldn't care if he ran off with our little girl. All they ever wanted was our money."

Joe placed a hand gently on Irene's arm, and leaned forward, capturing everyone's attention. "We believe she is safe. Her room appeared tidy and she left a note. We have just started this investigation and we won't rest until we have answers."

"It is late," Irene took over. "Please do not contact Miss Flaversham as we are now in charge of this case and the school knows the heaviness with which this issue lies. We require your telephone number should we need to be in touch. And we would like to interview any housekeepers or maids that have tended to Charlotte. Compile a list of your thoughts as well as the names of the staff we shall speak to and we will be by in the morning."

Mrs. Bancroft chimed in. "You are going to wait until morning?"

"What do you suppose we do – traipse around in the dark? We will be exhausted and useless, and then nothing will be done. Get us those names and any other information you can, and we will speak tomorrow."

* * * * *

It was nearing eleven o'clock that evening. Irene sat cross-legged on Joe's bed in his room across the hall from her own. Her eyes were shut tight as she worked through the clues from the day. A blanket she'd originally draped on her shoulders, now bunched around her like a nest.

Joe dug something out of his bag, causing the mattress to bend.

"You do have a room for yourself, you know."

She felt him tower over her, but her eyes remained closed. "Yes, but I have grown accustomed to your shuffling, and it soothes me when I need to think sometimes."

He made an impressed noise. "That's certainly a huge change from just last year when you would silence me—"

"Joe. I require your shuffling, not your commentary."

He chuckled. "Of course."

He continued to walk about the room, occasionally stopping and muttering something to himself. Finally, he came to stand over her again.

"I can't do much more. I'm at the stage where I change for bed."

"I'm not looking."

"Irene…"

"Fine, I shall go. I will see you at dawn."

Before she left Joe's room, his friend glanced at him, brow furrowed. "Did you ever run away from home when you were younger?"

"I can't recall. My house got overwhelming with my three sisters. I spent a lot of time in the barn or in the berry fields, but I don't think I ever intended to escape my family."

Irene nodded, taking in his words.

"Let me guess – you never thought to run because your father let you go anywhere you wished, whenever you wanted, and also gave you privacy for however long you needed."

"Correct. It didn't even occur to me once. And, if I should have any children, I will make sure that they never feel the need to run."

Joe grabbed the blanket from the bed to hand to Irene. "If you did have children, they'll certainly spend their days learning how to take over London, but will always come home, I'm sure of it. And if they need a break from you, they can always come hide upstairs in my room."

Irene quirked an eyebrow, a smile stretching across her whole face. "You will still be living upstairs even then?"

Joe realised his words and gave a sleepy chuckle. "Evidently. Now, go to bed. I feel tomorrow will be a long day full of keeping feuding parents away from each other."

He draped the blanket over her shoulders.

"Quite right. Goodnight, Joe."

* * * * *

The next morning, they headed back to the Bancroft estate. Hopefully, the new day would shed some more light on the case. She'd rung Madame Joffrey's school earlier, but there had been nothing to report.

The pair were not matching, with Irene opting for tan and green, while Joe stuck with brown. Though, as they drove, she noticed how the colours complemented each other.

Soon, they were welcomed back to the sitting area in the grand mansion.

The estate bustled in the daytime. Out of the large window, two gardeners were seen hard at work trimming the bushes. The smell of breakfast cooking in the kitchen and cleaning products from one of the dozen rooms wafted through the house.

Mr. and Mrs. Bancroft sat across from them. Irene noticed the puffy eyes and stifling yawns of them both and wondered if either of them got any sleep last night.

Joe started the questions with one she assumed he'd been dying to ask simply for himself. "This house is magnificent. Were you able to keep up with it all during the war?"

Mrs. Bancroft shook her head. "Sadly no. We had to let almost all the staff go. Nineteen-thirty-eight, was it? Too early, in my opinion. But half of them wanted to go away to war, and the others had siblings or lovers that were away. We just couldn't take the constant moaning about their safety. The house was restaffed again quite quickly once the war ended, and one of the maids we let go even came back. Her family didn't return, of course, but we weren't too concerned."

That detail piqued Irene's interest. A returning maid was usually either treated well or paid a nice sum. Despite the clout and funds the Bancroft's had, she couldn't see them doing either of those with their staff.

"This maid that you welcomed back, her family once worked for you?"

"Yes. But she was the only one to return."

"What happened to the rest?"

"I'm not sure, actually. It didn't matter to us. It was easier to have Rosa back than to hire someone new. She already knew the house layout and our expectations, though it had been a while. So, despite the barriers, we offered her the job."

"What barriers?"

Lighting a cigarette, Mrs. Bancroft waved her hand in the air. "She barely speaks English. I know some people say that Spanish is the language of love, but I cannot see why. Charlotte had even picked up phrases before the war. Singing songs that we couldn't even understand. We had to speak to Rosa's parents multiple times about it. But now she does an excellent job and we've never had to correct her."

"So, Rosa and her family worked here while Charlotte was growing up? Would they be around the same age?"

"The girl is two years older, but that doesn't matter when you're the help. Charlotte played with her all the same."

Irene stood abruptly, causing Joe to almost drop his pen in surprise. "We shall speak to Rosa now."

Mrs. Bancroft's eyes widened. "I'm sure she has nothing to do with it."

"Perhaps not, but if she grew up with Charlotte, then she may be able to share some things that not even you both know."

The couple both huffed at the insult, but the woman lit another cigarette. "In the mornings, she does all her mending and stitching before the meals begin. She is probably in her quarters. I can have someone fetch her—"

"No need," Irene cut him off. "Interviewing her in her own room is exactly what I want to do. If you'll point us in the right direction or have one of your staff lead us, that will be all we require. That, and a recent photograph of Charlotte, if you please."

An older gentleman with arms almost too long for his body led the sleuths to a lower room at the rear of the house. He silently gestured to the door before trudging away.

A moment after she knocked, Irene heard a hesitant "Yes?"

Rosa's room was larger than she'd expected. There was a bed and dresser at the back, and a grand sewing table at the forefront. Fabric and clothing lay all over the table and the small couch beside it. Bookshelves lined the one wall, stuffed with trinkets and photos.

The maid sat at the desk, peeking around a rather large machine. Upon Irene and Joe's entrance, she stood immediately and stumbled over an apology. "I'm sorry. Are you lost? Are you new staff?"

Her white dress was a tad frillier than a usual maid's. She was slight and unimposing, except for her brilliantly light blue eyes.

"Not at all. I am Irene Holmes and this is my colleague, Doctor Joe Watson."

"A doctor?" Rosa said, voice high. It was perforated by a thick Spanish accent. "I am not sick. Did Mr. Bancroft send for you?"

"Not at all. We're here to speak to you about Charlotte. May we sit? It won't take long."

Rosa nodded, her voluminous black curls bouncing as she cleared the small couch for them.

Irene took the opportunity to look around the busy space again. Bright reds and oranges decorated every corner; a small pocket of Spain tucked into an English estate. Jewellery covered the dresser, and from where she stood, Irene gleaned a few pieces too big for a woman to wear. Some men's rings, ornate in design, and a large cross that matched the delicate gold one Rosa wore around her neck. A pair of boots sat by the door with day-old mud caked to the heel. While Irene knew that Rosa probably went outside, for her to be traipsing through the gardens was certainly odd. The soil looked dark and rich as if from a flowerbed. Rosa was clearly the seamstress of the house, not part of the gardening staff and there were no more signs of workwear in the room.

Curious, but not yet suspicious.

Irene sat next to Joe while Rosa dragged her desk chair around.

"Charlotte has run away from her school," she started.

"Run away?"

"She climbed through a window and ran off in the middle of the night."

Rosa shook her head. "That does not make sense. She told me she loved going to that school. Every time she is home, she tells us how much she enjoys it there."

"You're correct. It doesn't make sense. And that's why we are here. You've known Charlotte for a long time."

Rosa nodded. As she spoke, her 'r's rolled in frustration. "We – me and my family – came to work for them just before the war. I played with Charlotte a lot. This house is big, and we were good at hide and seek. When the war came, they sent us all away."

"They hired you back, though," Irene offered.

"Only me. *Mi mama y papa* were too old to be of use to them." The girl's neck muscles tightened, and she tucked her hands together, subtly squeezing her thumb.

"What became of your parents?"

Rosa hesitated as if trying to translate her answer in her head. "They are doing fine. They have a small house in the country."

"These are your parents, correct?" Irene stood and grabbed a picture of a Spanish couple from a table near the bed. Her father was a short, older man with wide shoulders and a kind face. Meanwhile, the mother was a mirror image her daughter, with dark hair and pale eyes. They stood outside of a what appeared to be this very estate.

"Yes. I took it with the Bancroft's camera right before the war. I had to work extra to pay for the film I used. But I wanted a photograph of my parents so badly."

Irene handed her the picture and gave her another once-over. The girls' body language was hard to read. She looked scared and worried, with a furrowed brow and gaze darting everywhere. She also appeared angry, squeezing her thumb and clenching her jaw.

"Have you enjoyed working for the Bancrofts?"

"Yes." The answer came a little too quickly for Irene's liking. "They took me back in, even though Charlotte is not here. They give me a fine allowance to go into town. And now that I speak English, they let me off work for an afternoon when Charlotte comes to visit so I can spend time with her."

"What is she like?"

"What do you mean?"

Irene couldn't tell if she was stalling or simply didn't understand the question.

"Her demeanour." Irene said, then elaborated further as the woman stared at her. "Her personality. Is she nice? Mean? Would she stay at home or go out dancing often?"

"Ah, I understand. She was nice to everyone. And very...thoughtful. Her running away is strange. But we all do silly things when we are young."

"You are still young," Joe offered, speaking for the first time.

Rosa shot him a glare, then steeled herself. "I am, but I am not foolish. I would not want to make trouble, especially because I have this job."

"But you would tell us if Charlotte had come back home, even in secret, in the last two days?"

"Oh yes." She nodded, big black curls bouncing. "I would not wish trouble on her. She is a sweet girl."

Irene shifted gears as the pieces in the corner caught her eye again, namely the large ring and men's cross.

"What of this collection behind you? They are beautiful, but I will admit, my knowledge of the Spanish jewellery culture is subpar. Some of those appear to be big, like they belong to a man."

She looked at them and smiled fondly. "*Mi papa's*. He meant for me to sell some to get money for myself, but I could not let them go."

It took Rosa a second before her gaze returned to Irene. There were no sentimental tears in her eyes. Her thumb had turned dark red from squeezing the digit for the entire conversation.

Irene was inclined to believe her about the jewellery, for they matched the pieces her father had worn in the photograph. Still, she veered the discussion in another direction, a tactic she employed to catch someone off-guard.

"Do you know Tobias Clarke?"

Beside her, Joe paused, as he often did when she changed subjects so quickly, but he kept his pencil at the ready.

At the boy's name, Rosa stiffened and released her thumb. Her fingers curled in the fabric of her skirt, digging into her legs, in a subtle move that told Irene they had more than one run-in.

"I do know him. He was around a lot when we were younger. I did not like him."

"Why?"

"He was mean. Rude. Charlotte never liked him either, and when she would refuse him, he would turn his attention to me. And what am I to do as a simple maid?"

"He made passes at you?"

"He tried. Sometimes, he succeeded." The girl's brow darkened. At this point, she'd all but stretched a hole in her skirt.

Irene wanted to press for more information about Tobias, but feared the conversation would turn into nothing but slander, and she needed the maid focused on the task at hand.

"Is there anything else you can think of that will aid our investigation?"

"None right now. But I will tell Mr. or Mrs. Bancroft if I do."

"Thank you for your time." Irene stood.

"I will lead you out."

"No need. We remember the way, and we've kept you long enough from your chores."

Rosa gave them a small curtsy and headed back to her sewing.

As they made their way toward the front of the estate, Joe remarked, "I've never heard an accent like that. But what does that leave us with?"

"A sour reputation of Tobias Clarke," Irene said, pausing at one of the dozens of small tables lining the halls. This one had a small vase balancing on a lacy doily. "If this man is as bad as everyone says, then Charlotte has run away by herself, perhaps even to escape him."

"I feel like we've just opened up more questions."

"Let's focus on Lizzie now. If only because her disappearance deserves as much attention, and to give us a break from Charlotte. So far, we assumed they fled separately, but there is a chance that they became odd friends and left together."

Chapter IV

Sorting Through the Nightly Visitors

While not as grand as the Bancroft's, Lizzie Roberts hailed from a large estate, with small wings on either side. Gardeners were busy planting flowers from dozens of wheelbarrows along the front gardens.

Joe and Irene were led through the double doors with stained glass and into yet another sitting room set up very much like the last one; even boasting the same cluster of expensive objects, trinkets, and drapery that probably cost more than Joe could even count to.

Mr. and Mrs. Roberts settled at opposite ends of the couch, very much as if they hated each other. Where the man was short and well-fed, his wife was tall, lithe, and had on at least a few layers of make-up.

She leaned forward, pointing her cigarette holder at Irene. "Before we start, I want to make it perfectly clear that we contributed to several charities and gave plenty to the war effort over the years."

From his friend's sour expression, Joe knew this interview would be curt. His sole purpose here would be to keep her from running her mouth.

"Why would I care what money you've donated?"

Mr. Roberts tapped his cigarette. "Isn't that why you're here? To investigate our earnings?"

"No. We are here about your daughter, Lizzie."

The woman rolled her eyes. "What has she done now?"

"She has run away from her school, it appears."

Both parents exchanged exasperated looks with one another. Mrs. Roberts was the first of them to speak, her tone lacklustre and bored.

"Sounds like something she'd do. I thought someone might have snatched her up by now. But if she's run, then maybe she'll finally be happy wherever she ends up."

The lack of care shocked Joe. He and Irene had dealt with detached parents before, but the children had never been in danger. Beside him, Irene fumed. He could practically feel the heat resonate from her body.

"You don't speak fondly of your daughter."

Mr. Roberts grabbed another cigarette, offering one to the doctor, but he shook his head. The man was done speaking for now, allowing his wife to take over the conversation.

"She was nothing but trouble. She had dreams of working in London."

"I work in London." Irene's words were still clipped. Joe prepared to calm her and hoped that the older couple didn't instigate further.

"Some people have no choice." Mrs. Roberts looked down her nose.

"I feel privileged to work."

"Lizzie never had to. And yet, she rebelled at every opportunity. You should've seen her during the war. Running around the streets at fourteen like some hooligan."

"People tend to run when bombs are falling around them."

It was time. Joe placed a hand on Irene's shoulder, but it didn't work its usual magic. She didn't relax at all. Seeing that more complicated tactics would be needed here, he gave a small squeeze and hurried to speak.

"We would like to find Lizzie. If not for your sake, then for hers. Other than being a rebel, is there any reason why she would have to run away from school? In turn, did she ever mention anyone coming around to visit or anything that might indicate where she'd gone?"

"She never wrote home. I counted on the monthly reports from the headmistress to let us know she was still there."

"Is there anything unique about your daughter that may help her stand out?"

"She has a shellfish allergy."

"That's not..." Joe trailed off.

"May we have the most recent photograph you have of her?" Irene finally spoke, tone restrained and professional.

Mrs. Roberts waved her hand and glanced at their butler. He returned with a photo box in record time. Neither host made any move to take it, and he set it on a high table at the side of the room. After a minute of rifling through the contents, he handed Irene a picture.

Lizzie was a thin girl, with long dark hair and a sour expression. Irene gave the item to Joe to stick it his notebook. She then stood, clearly done with this interview.

"If Lizzie comes by, ring the hotel in town immediately. You may not care, but we would like to find her."

Mrs. Roberts waved her hand as she lit yet another cigarette.

The butler gestured for Joe and Irene to follow him out of the house. As they walked across the gravel drive back to their car, Joe sighed.

"They were quite unpleasant. And it's alarming how little they care for their daughter."

Irene paused before climbing into the Vauxhall. "When this is finished, I may put an investigator onto their earnings, simply out of spite."

* * * * *

Irene parked in front of the rather nice hotel they were staying at and they started down the street. Their first stop was a bakery that, despite the shortages that still lingered from the war, smelled incredible. Unfortunately, the baker hadn't seen either girl.

Next was a flower shop where the owner said she was too busy to notice any teenagers, but was almost certain they hadn't come by.

After more dead ends, the pair ended up at the pub across from the hotel. Though small, the inside of the building was bursting with energy on this particular Friday afternoon.

The barkeep handed a working man a pint, then smiled as Irene approached. "Hello, love. What can I get you?"

"Answers, hopefully." She held up the photos. "Have you seen either of these young women in the past two days?"

He inspected both pictures before pointing to Charlotte. "Haven't seen her, but the skinny one with the dark hair I have. She came in here waving money around and bought a few drinks and a meal. A fellow sat down next to her and they chatted."

"Go on," Irene urged as Joe tucked the pictures away. "Do not leave out any details."

The man sighed and eyed the other patrons in the bar. Irene didn't care if he was busy. She waved her hand, encouraging him to continue.

"He was a regular, of sorts. I see him once a week but don't know his name. Nice fellow, never complained. Dark hair, a bit on the skinny side, had a green coat on. I didn't think much of it as they seemed to get on quite well. Then the girl suggested they leave together. I like to consider myself a decent man, so when she walked by, I asked her if all was good. She nodded her head genuine-like. So, I didn't bother after that."

"Did you see which way they went when they left?"

"Didn't think to look."

"Thank you," Irene sighed. "May we have some chips, please?"

"Sure, love." The barkeep turned to call back to the kitchen as Joe closed his notebook.

"Do we pursue Lizzie?"

"There's no point. She's long gone by now. But we will have Scotland Yard put out a notice should anyone see her. I suspect that she's tough, given her description. Charlotte's case seems more delicate, so we shall focus on it for the time being. Now, grab the chips and let's go back to our hotel."

A group of men at a table by the door let out a few low whistles as Irene walked past them.

One of them called to Joe. "Got yourself a firecracker, didn't you?"

"I'd sure love to grab those chips fast and follow her right to that hotel, you lucky fella," another one chimed in.

Joe humoured them with a chuckle as the barkeep came back with the food. Little did they know that was his exact plan, but for reasons entirely out of their imagination.

Just the mere thought of what they were suggesting made his cheeks warm. He usually could ignore people's thoughts on his and Irene's bond, but the occasional worry slipped through. It made him truly aware of just how unique their friendship was, and how it was perceived.

He was so lost in his own thoughts that when he left the pub he smacked right into Irene.

"The chips!" She cried and stuck her hands out, but Joe held the basket steady. "That could've been a disaster!"

With the crisis averted, they started across the street. A jingling sound came from Irene as she bounced along.

"What do you have in your bag?" Joe asked, trying to see if the shape of her satchel gave it away.

"What do you mean?"

"You're clinking. I also noticed it when you leaned on the bar, and when you were looking at the big bouquet of roses at the flower shop."

She didn't answer, but a sly smirk fluttered across her lips as they headed down the pavement toward the hotel.

"Irene, what did you do?"

"Nothing that will be noticed."

"You are emptying your bag as soon as we get in."

"Doctor Watson," she gasped. "A woman's purse is sacred and secret."

He snorted. "That's not your *purse*. That's your investigation bag left over from the first war. There are several weapons and detective kits in there. And something clinking. Considering we've been to a dozen places with glass and metal objects, I'm sure it's something you should not have."

She stopped and held the bag out for him. "You're right, I do carry all our equipment. Perhaps you should take a turn."

Joe squared his shoulder, trying to keep the amusement from his face. "I have my own bag."

"Full of what? A notebook and wallet?"

"Yes."

Irene kept holding out her satchel, pulling her lips into a tight line, clearly to keep from laughing. He called her bluff and swiped it from her, switching it for the chips, which she gladly held. He slung it over his free shoulder.

"I look like a pack mule."

"A tall, slender, handsome pack mule, though. Now, let's be off!"

She skipped down the pavement, smiling back at him.

Joe started after her, bags bumping both hips.

* * * * *

He stared at the pile of trinkets on his bed. Two ashtrays, a small vase, half a dozen decorative marbles, and a photograph of who could only be Tobias Clarke, were spread out on the blanket. Irene had taken objects before from places they'd travelled, but never this many.

"You have to give these back. Especially this picture."

His partner sat cross-legged beside the collection, fingers steepled, eyes closed. The half-eaten basket of chips was perched in front of her and every now and then, she'd shove one in her mouth.

"They won't even miss them."

"That's not the point."

She opened her eyes and glanced at the pile, then at him. "I'll give the picture back when we are done with the investigation. But the others I am keeping."

She ate another chip.

Joe knew there was no more point in arguing anymore. "May I have one of those before you devour them all?"

Irene grabbed a chip from the basket and held it out, eyes still closed. He refrained from telling her he could've taken his own as he plucked it from her fingers and popped it in his mouth, waiting for a direction.

"Read me what you've written about Charlotte's visitor."

"All the descriptions?" Joe said, reaching for his notebook.

"Everything you have in the order you wrote them. But first, give me a piece of paper and a pencil for myself. And one of those books off the shelf to write on."

Joe did as asked. As soon as she had everything, Irene hunched over the book, pencil in hand, still cross-legged. He sat on the small bed with her, if only to be close to the chips before she finished them.

"Short hair. Long hair. Dark hair. Short, light hair. Bald. Big, dark helmet. Dark eyes. Light eyes. Light eyes and dark hair. Cropped hair and dark eyes. Red hair – though that might have been me. Broad shoulders. Short. Tall. Tall with broad shoulders. Short with a thick neck. Then we move on to hands. They certainly said a lot about hands... and hair. I didn't know those things were so important to women. Anyway. Large hands, which received a lot of giggles. Long fingers with rings. Short fingers with no rings. Then they all started asking about my hands and that's when it devolved into chaos."

He looked up at Irene. She scribbled on her piece of paper like a madwoman, eyes flying over the words. Finally, she sat straight and looked upon her work, giving a satisfied nod. She'd written two columns and separated the descriptors into each:

<u>Tobias Clarke</u>	<u>Boy #2</u>
Short, light hair	Long, dark and wavy hair
Dark eyes	Light eyes
Short	Broad shoulders
Thick neck	Long fingers with rings
Short fingers	Tall
No rings	

"There were two boys!" She cried. "Half of those obviously describe Tobias, but the others all point to a completely different person."

Joe stared at the lists. She was correct, of course, but this opened a whole new list of suspects.

Irene leapt from the bed, tipping the chip basket all over the blanket. Ignoring the mess, she paced, thinking aloud.

"But which one did she leave with? We need to go back to the school and see if any of the girls had brothers. Or at least get clarity on this other man. I should've asked them more questions. I should not have assumed they would simply offer up someone they knew."

"Shall we visit the school tonight?" Joe asked, collecting the spilled chips.

"Perhaps. We—"

Small but heavy footsteps sounded down the hallway, then a

sharp knock came from the door.

"Mr. Holmes! Mrs. Holmes! Are you in there? An urgent telephone call came for you."

Joe dumped the chips into the basket and rushed to the door, flinging it open. The young boy from the hotel kitchen stood in the hallway, face red and out of breath.

"It's the madame from some school."

Irene headed straight downstairs, pushing past both of them. Joe mumbled an apology to the kid who kept trying to repeat his message.

The telephone was at the small front desk near the door, off its receiver, waiting for them. Irene scooped it up, and Joe tucked in close, stooping to listen in on the call.

"Irene Holmes speaking."

"Miss Holmes. It's Miss Flaversham," her voice was shaky and hurried. "They've found a body. The groundskeepers. In a shed near the back forest. It's a large shed. It's a man's body. Well, a young man. A large young man—"

"Miss Flaversham," Irene cut her off, taking control of the conversation. "Listen to me. Let no one near the body and do not ring the police. Keep all the girls in the school, even if they are set to go home this weekend. Keep the groundskeeper in your office and do not let him speak with anyone. I shall interview him when I arrive."

"Please hurry, Miss Holmes. It appears this body has been

here for quite some time. It smells something fierce!"

Irene hung up, grinning from ear to ear. "The game's afoot now, my dear Joe! Murders do make things much more interesting!"

She skipped toward the stairs. Joe glanced around at the other patrons milling about the lobby and gave a small wave of apology before following his friend upstairs.

Chapter V

The Identity of the Body in the Shed

Irene drove to the edge of Madame Joffrey's backfield. She thought about taking the vehicle farther, but didn't quite trust the soft grass. She and Joe exited the car, and she immediately sighed.

"What part of 'stay at the school' did she not understand?"

Miss Flaversham stood by the large shed near the treeline with a larger man in overalls. Hopefully they kept their fingers off the crime scene.

"It's fine." Joe sensed her frustration, as usual. "I'm sure they stayed away."

Annette emerged into the field as well as if she had been waiting behind the building for them to arrive. "Hello, Miss Holmes! I was wondering if you needed any help at all?"

Irene startled and stepped back into Joe, who steadied her. "Uh, no. Not right now."

"Okay. Sorry to scare you. This is just the most exciting thing that has happened here. We all liked Charlotte and want to help."

"I will let you know." Irene gave the enthusiastic girl an encouraging nod, if only to get her to move on and stop interrupting their case. She then started across the field once more. Her shoes sunk into the soft grass, confirming the sound decision to wear her heavier boots.

Her partner danced beside her, avoiding puddles. "Were you that eager when you were young?"

"Of course. But never that obvious about it."

As they approached the headmistress, she gave them a small, curt wave but stayed next to the rather pudgy man. In turn, he stared at the ground with a face almost as green as the grass.

"Oh, thank goodness," Miss Flaversham said. "No one's touched him. I—"

Irene turned directly to the groundskeeper. "You found him?"

He nodded. "I didn't go in the shed, Miss, I promise. I just opened it and saw him laying there. We rarely use this shed, see, but I needed some tools to fix that bush around the corner. It was overgrown and—"

"Thank you. Please stand near that large tree and be ready to answer questions should I need you."

The man nodded, all too eager to step away.

Irene immediately crouched to survey the ground. "Miss

Flaversham, you may join him. I don't like anyone hovering while I investigate."

"Oh, yes." The elegant woman sounded slightly offended, but took a few steps back nevertheless.

With people out of the way, Irene began her investigation. "Ready to scribe, Doctor?"

"Of course." She heard him dig his notebook out.

Still crouched, she waddled toward the shed. "No footprints, ground's too soft, but flattened grass suggests much foot traffic. That stench is quite ugly. Whomever is in there has been dead for a while."

The doors were closed but not locked; the groundskeeper must've let them shut on their own in his shock. The structure itself was about the size of a small bedroom, three meters by three meters. Before stepping inside, Irene poked through the grass, standing the strands up. There was a dark spot, then another beside it.

Gooey to the touch.

Blood.

The drops were hard to find, but through sheer determination, they led her a few strides away and into the woods. Irene straightened and called to Miss Flaversham.

"What's on the other side of these trees?"

"Farms," the headmistress replied. "And then another town. Are you going to go into the—"

Irene pivoted to the shed, ignoring the woman. The metal lock was smashed and thrown in the grass. She opened the doors and the smell hit her like a wave. It truly was something fierce. Taking a small step back, she sucked in fresh air and dug a torch from her bag.

A stocky young man was sprawled out on the dirt floor. Burlap sacks from a knocked-over shelf concealed the face. Gardening tools were strewn around as well, a clear sign of struggle.

Tossing the burlap to side, Irene shone her light on the dead man.

Tobias Clarke III was face up, eyes blown open, as coagulated blood soaked the dirt beneath his head.

"It's been at least twenty-four hours." She noted the bloat and deep red and blue pooling at the bottom of the arms.

"That coincides with the night Charlotte went missing," Joe offered from the door as he scrawled in his book.

Careful not to shift any more props or leave too much of a mark, Irene stepped toward Tobias' shoulders, slipping her gloves on at the same time. Then, as gently as she could, she lifted his bloated head off of a large, jagged rock. A chunk was missing from his scalp.

"Did he fall?"

She didn't answer. Instead, she laid Tobias' head down in the dirt before scooping up the blood-covered rock. It was hefty, big enough to hold with both hands. She turned it over. Blood covered both sides; on the bottom was a small explosion of droplets and the other side sported an oozing pattern.

"He was hit on the back of the head. He didn't fall as the scene suggests."

There was definitely a scuffle between Tobias and another assailant, but she couldn't tell who.

Irene gently lifted Tobias' arm as she circled toward him again. A large, bloodied army knife sat in the dirt. She picked it up to examine. The blood from the head wound didn't reach the knife, which meant…

She searched the puffed up body. "Curious."

Joe must've caught up to her thoughts, because he scribbled away. "He wasn't stabbed, was he?"

Irene shook her head.

"Whose blood is on the knife, then?"

"Whose indeed."

Was it one attacker? Two? Was Tobias the instigator, or was someone waiting for him in here?

"No blood drops behind him," Irene thought out loud. "But there *is* blood in front of him. So, two attackers. Or defenders."

There was no room to pace, but she lowered her head anyway to take even three steps back and forth. As she moved forward, something else caught her eye. A small white dot in the dirt.

She crouched and plucked a pearl earring from near Tobias' hip.

"Oh no," Joe muttered. She heard him flipping through his notebook. Charlotte was wearing the exact piece in the picture they had.

"It's time to phone Eddy." She sent Joe away and waved Miss Flaversham over.

The woman came running. "Who is in there? Oh, heavens!" She reacted with her whole body – first to the earring, then to the corpse.

"It is Tobias Clarke. I need to you ring Scotland Yard and ask for DI Lestrade specifically. Tell him Irene has asked for him; that it's a very particular emergency for his eyes only. Do not speak to anyone else and keep the girls away. We have already spoken to the girls' parents, and they will hear from only Joe and I moving forward. Understood?"

To the headmistress's credit, she was as cooperative as they went. She squared her shoulders and nodded.

"Excellent. We'll be back. Come, Joe!"

She pivoted and started around the shed, spotting the blood trail again in the grass. As she followed the blood trail in the grass, though, a heavy regret settled over her like a weighted blanket. Reviewing the timeline of the murder, Irene grew frustrated at her incompetence. She stopped just inside the treeline, causing Joe to bump into her.

"Irene? You alright?"

"Oh, Joe. How could I be such an idiot?"

He stepped around her to catch her eye. "What are you talking about?"

"We should've searched the shed," she said, running through the many things she should have done since the beginning of this case. "We should've looked everywhere on the property for clues!"

"We were interviewing suspects."

"I am slipping, Joe. I am losing my touch."

"Where is this coming from, Irene? You aren't losing your touch. We're just two people."

"Two people who do everything together! We should've split up. We should have—"

"We didn't, though," her partner said, grasping her shoulders. "We can't change that right now. What we can do is follow this blood trail to hopefully more clues, right?"

She wasn't listening. "On some of our cases last year, we were so on top of things and quick thinkers. But, this case and the last…"

He gently grabbed her chin, tilting it up so she looked at him. "The winter was rough. We are still amateurs—"

"You are."

"So are you. There's a difference between helping Scotland Yard solve their crimes during a war and taking on exuberant mysteries on your own. I'm sure your father made plenty of mistakes when he was starting out."

"Highly unlikely."

"Listen to me, Irene, I would love to talk all of this out once we are back at Baker Street. But right now, we owe it to Charlotte and Lizzie to find them. So, tuck this away and focus on the case."

She wanted to argue and point out every single flaw and how she *had* failed, but Joe was right. This was no time for no silly feelings. Dwelling upon her mistakes wouldn't do. There'd be time for that once it was all over.

"Alright. Back to the case." Irene flipped the switch on her emotions. Rolling her shoulder, she crouched once again to pick up the trail.

They went in through the woods, shining a torch along their path. Away from the soggy grass, there was a clear trail to follow. Flattened plants and snapped twigs, mixed with the occasional blood drop or two, made it very easy.

Soon they emerged at a rickety fence separating a farmer's small field and the trees behind. There was a break in the fence from years past, and Irene studied the splintered wood. A bloodied handprint was smeared on the roughened surface, too large to belong to Charlotte.

A six-box barn sat at the top of the shallow hill. Irene hurried forward, vaguely aware of Joe shouting something to her about trespassing on private property. The barn's back door was latched, but as she pushed on the wood, the only sound in the air was that of a quiet tinkle of metal. She snatched a business card from her bag and slid it up between the door and wall, smiling in satisfaction as the hook popped out of the eye.

There was no blood by the door, but off to the right, toward the first stall, a dark spot caught her attention. This box, unlike the others, was void of straw or hay. There were deep red smears on the side panels, but none on the floor.

Behind her, Joe panicked. "We are trespassing, Irene. I'm going up to the house to let someone know we are—"

The front door burst open.

A shotgun cocked behind them.

"Stay right where you are."

Irene turned to the gruff, angry voice. Beside her, Joe faced forward, arms up, muscles stiff.

An older gentleman with worn overalls aimed his weapon at Irene. His finger was off the trigger, however, and she doubted that there was ammo in the gun.

"I'm Irene Holmes and this is Doctor Joe Watson. We are private investigators. You won't need that weapon. We're harmless. Where did the straw from this box go?"

The farmer hesitated for an excruciating moment before lowering the gun, but still kept a wary eye on her. "I took it out."

"Because it was covered in blood."

He slowly nodded, his fingers relaxing on the shotgun.

Irene shifted on her feet, annoyed that she had to drag a

conversation out.

"Like I said, we are investigators trying to solve a missing person case. Please, tell us what happened here."

Propping the gun on his hip, barrel toward the ground, the man pulled a pack of cigarettes from his pocket. He stuck one in his mouth. "I heard a commotion early yesterday morning and found a young couple. The boy was bleeding. I wasn't having any of it, so I sent them away into town to get a doctor."

Before she had to ask, Joe dug out the picture of Charlotte. "Was this her?"

He stepped closer to look at the picture, then nodded. "Yeah, that was her."

"What about the boy – what did he look like?"

"The boy was a Spaniard. Had a heavy accent. Long hair."

"And it was him that was injured?" Irene's heart picked up as she leaped to different scenarios.

"Sure was. Bled all over my stall."

"Did it appear like the girl was forced to travel with him?"

"Not at all. She worried about him a whole lot. Don't know more than that, though. I told them to scram as quick as they could."

"Where's the doctor's office?"

The farmer gave a nod toward the front. "Just in town, second building in."

Irene took off past him, a new objective in mind. They were a day behind Charlotte and this mystery man.

There was no time to lose.

Luckily, the town was only a ten-minute walk from the farmer's house. Irene easily spotted the few drops of blood on the light coloured road. Soon they walked along the pavement right to the second building when she abruptly stopped.

Joe gently collided with her. "That was a quick trip. So sorry, Irene. I was thinking about this Spanish man. Do you think Rosa knows him? No one has mentioned anyone resembling him except for the girls who saw him outside Charlotte's window."

"There are half a dozen scenarios. Let's see what this doctor says, then we will ponder. But right now, we will keep moving forward. An object in motion remains in motion and all of that."

He raised an eyebrow. "Are you talking about Newton's Law?"

"Of course." She stepped up toward the doctor's office, the doorbell jingling above her.

Inside, a secretary stood at a tall file cabinet, folders in her hands. "So sorry, we're just about to close for the day. You didn't have an appointment, did you?"

"No." Irene produced the roughed business card she had used to open the barn door previously. "I am Irene Holmes and this is Doctor Watson. A young woman and an injured man came through here yesterday morning. We are investigators and must know everything about them."

"The man with the blue eyes?"

"Yes."

The woman put the folders down. "Follow me into the surgery while I fetch the doctor."

She led them into a clean room to wait. Irene drummed her fingers on the counter, annoyed and frustrated with herself that they were so behind.

Meanwhile, Joe was in his element. He took to the shelves of medical tools and books, poking and prodding out of curiosity.

He picked up a small, wrapped packet. "That's one thing we don't have at home. Hopefully, I never have to stitch up one of us in an emergency, but it would be nice to have it at Baker Street."

"He certainly has enough of them." Irene eyed the stack.

Just then the doctor – a tired-looking man in his late forties – finally entered. "Miss Holmes and Doctor Watson, I presume? Nice to see a fellow medical man."

"I'm a veterinarian," Joe said, shaking his hand.

"Ah, well done! Could never handle the animals myself, but they're probably easier to deal with than some humans."

"Quite right."

Irene cleared her throat, swallowing a snide remark about the timetable of a missing girl. The men took the hint.

The doctor continued speaking. "You're here to discuss the young couple I aided earlier, correct?"

He focused on Joe after giving Irene a wary look. She had no idea what her expression was, but most probably her eyebrows were furrowed and her jaw taught.

"That's correct," Joe answered the man.

"Now, as a doctor yourself, you can understand that I can't disclose any information—"

Time was of the essence, and this man was wasting it. Irene cut in. "Yes, we know. Though it may be a case of kidnapping."

This gave him pause. "It certainly didn't seem that way."

"The girl is not yet eighteen years old. Still a child." She showed him Charlotte's photo.

A sweat bead appeared on his forehead and the man shifted on his feet. "I didn't know. She said she was older than that. I do not wish to get Scotland Yard involved. I was simply helping them. It was all innocent, I promise."

"If it is so innocent, please tell us what happened. Start with a description of the man."

"He couldn't have been older than twenty-three and had long dark hair, tan skin, and these big, bright blue eyes like a deer's. He'd been stabbed in the side. They told me something about a kitchen accident, but even they knew it didn't sound the most believable. So, they also offered an obscene amount of money."

"Did they have it with them?"

She felt Joe stare at her; he was surely puzzled.

The doctor gave her the same look. "She had a hundred

pounds on her, but told me she could get me more."

"Curious. Continue."

He looked at the ground, sheepish.

Irene spoke again, if only to hurry the conversation. "You took the pounds, clearly, as you're wearing a new pair of shoes and I see that the jacket hanging through that window there still has the tags on it."

"I did, yes," the doctor stammered. "But I refused the rest she promised. I cleaned the boy up, stitched him, then they went on their way. They seemed madly in love, if that's any help."

"No names?"

"None, and they spoke to each other in Spanish."

"Which way did they go?"

Silence. A beat passed, then another. On the third, the man spoke up, "They asked to leave through the back door."

"And you let them?"

"I did. I had no reason to think—"

"One of them was stabbed," Irene snapped. "It didn't occur to you that there may be an issue?"

"I asked. But all they said was they were messing about in the kitchen, that's all. I didn't press even though I was sceptical. The wound was superficial, and jutted to the side of the rib cage, hardly the mark of a fight. So, I decided to give them the benefit of the doubt. This is a small town, located in a very wealthy community, and we don't get very many criminals or scandals. I mostly treat a child's occasional broken arm, common colds, or women's ailments."

Noting her growing displeasure, Joe placed a gentle hand on Irene's forearm. She shuffled back and took a few breaths, reluctantly letting him take over the conversation.

"We understand that this is an odd circumstance, and that you have certain rules with your patients, but if you could offer any other information, we would truly appreciate it."

"There isn't much more, I'm afraid. They entered, I stitched the boy up, he took a packet of pain pills, then they left out the back door. You are more than welcome to go through there and look in the alleyway."

Irene motioned for the doctor to lead the way.

He seemed surprised at the abrupt end to the conversation, but stepped out. Irene let her partner follow first as she had her eye on a shiny packet of tools sitting in the open cupboard. As the two men went out of sight, she tucked the item into her bag and hurried to catch up.

They exited the building into the small alleyway, barren of anything but cobblestones and some pebbles. There weren't even any windows from the surrounding buildings to offer a witness.

The man muttered something akin to a goodbye, to which Joe replied.

Irene ignored them, crouching to find any sort of clue, but

nothing turned up. She started out of the alleyway and looked both ways, yet came up empty-handed once again.

"This is smaller than the town on the other side of the school," Joe offered. "I wonder how long it will take them to converge as both populations grow."

Irene didn't know and didn't care. She sat down against the bakery next door and stifled a yawn. Her mind raced, but all of her solutions were guesses and assumptions, which she didn't like to abide if she could help it. How was she so rubbish with this? Was it because she hadn't dealt with a missing person before? Her cases had been mostly stalkers, and puzzles, and murders.

Joe sat beside her and patted her arm. "I suppose it's back to Rosa. The Spanish population around here can't be that large. Perhaps she knows this Spaniard."

Irene pushed a stone with her foot. "There has to be more clues somewhere. Two women and a man have been gallivanting in this area and no one has seen or heard anything!"

"We'll get someone to drive us back to the school and head to the Bancroft's. We will find them, Irene." Joe hopped up and extended his hand to her. "Or at least, we'll get some answers. We always get answers, right?"

She took his hand and stood, sighing. "You are correct. Let's go."

Chapter VI

Another Conversation with Señorita Rosa

This time Mrs. Bancroft answered the door herself, beckoning them in. "Well? What news?"

"No news yet," Irene said. "But we are in the midst of solving it. I have a couple of questions if you would so oblige."

"Of course, we can move into the sitting room—"

"No need. Right here will do."

Joe cringed, but the wealthy woman didn't seem to mind. Her husband appeared from around the corner and strode up to them. But before he could speak, Irene started in with her interrogation.

"Were there any other Spanish members you hired to work for you?"

"Yes," Mrs. Bancroft said. "We had an overabundance of help because they all fled Spain before the war."

"Then you let them *all* go in thirty-eight?"

"Yes. There were so many and they were all having children."

Irene snorted in disgust. "You speak of *them* as if they are a herd of cattle."

The woman waved her off. "Oh, of course not. There was just a lot of them."

"Right. We're going to speak with Rosa now."

Irene looked to the butler, who nodded at her. "She is in her room. I shall fetch her."

"Don't bother." The sleuth strode ahead. "We won't be but a minute."

"Would you not prefer one of our sitting rooms?" Mrs. Bancroft called after her.

Paying her no mind, Irene kept going.

"So sorry," she heard Joe sputter out the apology. "Time is of the essence."

Irene was determined; a new fire lit under her. How she knew the way back to Rosa's room was a mystery, as all the halls in this house looked the same to Joe. After a few twists and turns, though, they stopped at a door that seemed vaguely familiar.

A soft "Yes?" came as an answer to Irene's sharp knock. She didn't wait for a formal invitation, striding right inside.

Joe made a mental note to discuss the action of barging in on places when this case was over. The barn was one thing, but a woman's bedroom? No amount of frustration was an excuse.

Rosa leapt to her feet.

Irene waved her hands. "Calm down. I don't mean to intrude, but we have a few questions."

"I told you everything. I promise. I know nothing more!" The girl nervously stuttered out her words.

"Sit," Irene commanded.

For the briefest of moments, Rosa looked ready to fight back, but thought better and took a seat at her sewing desk. Joe sat opposite her, his cheeks warming from embarrassment.

His partner didn't appear to have such scruples; she stayed standing. Her eyes travelled all around the room, head swivelling in curiosity as she asked her questions.

"Charlotte was travelling with a Spaniard. We have it on good authority that they knew each other well. Now, the Spanish community cannot be that big, especially in a town of such a small population. The boy is about your age, fit, with long hair. Do you happen to know anyone like this?"

During their first interview, Rosa had seemed caught off guard, just like she'd been at the beginning of this intrusion. As Irene spoke, though, an eery calm settled over her features. She never made eye contact, but her voice was even.

"I don't think so, sorry."

"Of course." Irene strode to the bookshelf of trinkets near the window.

Joe scribbled down every observation he could, including the cool look of annoyance that passed over Rosa's features and her blink-and-you'll-miss-it glare. His partner didn't say anything more for a moment and the maid finally set her shoulders with a small huff.

"Did you come here to just look through my things? To be nosy?"

Irene turned to her, an innocent smile on her face. "Of course not. Tell me this: were your parents angry that only you were invited back to this house?"

Rosa took a second to answer. She grabbed a shawl and draped it over her shoulders.

"No. They had decided to stay in the country with the little bit of money they had. I know they did not want me to return, but what else would I do?"

"What indeed." Irene plucked a picture of the girl's parents.

Joe took the lull in conversation to attempt a quick observation of his own. A man's jewellery, and next to it, two dolls. He'd passed over them the previous time, but perhaps they were worth noting. A male and a female, handmade, both with bright blue buttons for eyes.

Again, nothing unusual for a woman to keep childhood toys.

He glanced up at the bookshelf and a volume caught his eye. This particular title was on poisonous flowers and plants. Next to it were a few books on gardening. Their spines were sticking out slightly – either they were used often or had recently been returned to the shelf.

He looked back at Rosa, attempting not to blush as he gave her a quick once-over. Small patches of dried mud caked the bottom of her skirt, and there was a pair of muddied boots in the corner of the room.

Joe felt puzzle pieces snapping together in his mind. But there was still one missing.

A maid with poison? It was almost too cliche.

Irene's voice drew him from his thoughts. "And what of your brother? Did he stay with your parents or venture off somewhere?"

Rosa immediately stiffened. "Brother? I don't—"

"He must be close in age," Irene continued, then picked up the dolls. "Perhaps a twin."

"I have no brother."

Joe interjected suddenly, feeling exactly like his friend when she acquired new information. He understood a bit better why she blurted things out. "Where are you growing your poisonous garden?"

Irene shot him a sly, proud smirk.

"I'm not growing anything," the girl affirmed, a bit too strongly.

"Mud on your skirt and shoes, books on poisonous plants, on gardening…" Joe trailed off. Now it felt like he was attacking the poor woman as she stared in distress.

His partner, however, continued for him. "Dirt under your

fingernails and a callous on your thumb. Not to mention the instant sweat and your shallow breathing as we are now questioning you on these particulars."

"I-I don't..."

Irene folded her arms expectantly.

As Joe watched Rosa, something occurred to him. If the maid was waiting for Charlotte to return home – to poison her or not – attacking her wouldn't do any good. If they spooked her into fleeing the scene, then they might lose Charlotte and the man she travelled with. Or worse, Rosa might seek them out and cause them harm. He stepped forward, ready to grab Irene's wrist, but as if reading his mind, she stopped talking. Glancing at him for a split second, she let out a great sigh and sauntered back.

"Perhaps we are being a bit hasty. And making things up because we are at our wit's end with this case. I apologise, Rosa." Her eyes downturned in rue. "We are jumping to all sorts of conclusions and delving into businesses that aren't our own. I, myself, have ventured into poisonous plants with no intention of harming anyone. We are simply trying to appease the rich folk." At her last sentence, Irene sunk into the couch. "Please forgive us. You can imagine the pressure we are under to return the princess to the castle."

Joe held his breath. The act was so believable, almost frighteningly so.

Rosa finally sighed. "It is okay. We are all worried."

Abruptly, as if recharged with a lightning rod, Irene stood and stuck out her hand to the woman. "Wonderful! Thank you for understanding. Have a wonderful evening, Rosa. And if Charlotte does come home, please ring us at the hotel and we can put this case to bed."

"Of course. I will show you out."

"Oh, no. We've taken up enough of your time. We've also visited enough that we know our way by now. Please go back to your work. And, how would you say 'good evening' in Spanish?"

"*Buenas noches*," Rosa provided..

"Well, *buenas noches*... Uh, *senorita?*"

"*Si, muy bueno.*"

Irene smiled and left the room.

Joe followed, giving a polite nod to Rosa as he went. He shut the door behind him and hurried to catch up to his friend.

They passed by a sitting room and Irene turned in, marching up to Mr. and Mrs. Bancroft sipping their tea.

Before she could speak, the woman lashed out. "Did Rosa have anything to do with this?"

"No," Irene lied. "We just wanted to clear something up. However, we have another suspect that we will pursue tonight. We are extremely close to getting your daughter back."

"Wonderful," Mrs. Bancroft said, continuing with her tea.

Irene whirled around, rolled her eyes at Joe, and headed out.

Once in the cool evening air, she finally spoke. "Joe, please tell me you have the same thought I do."

"That she would run if we accused her?"

She nodded as they reached the Vauxhall. "And she might act if we revealed her plan."

"By act, you mean harm Charlotte or her own brother."

"Yes."

"And she may jump to poison god knows who."

"Exactly."

"So, what do we do?"

Irene started the engine. "We wait."

"Wait?"

She nodded. "Charlotte has no money on her as she gave what she had to the doctor. Even if she or Rosa's brother did have money, they wouldn't risk going to a shop. She is a careful and clever girl. And, with this murder in their minds, they need to escape fast. I guarantee the couple will come back here for supplies. It's very easy to sneak into an estate like this one."

"And what are we to do? Sit in the woods and spy on the house?"

Her smile gave him the answer. "But first, we have other matters. Eddy should have arrived by now."

* * * * *

By the time they returned to the school, the sun had set enough for Irene to turn on the headlights. Scotland Yard's vehicles were parked down by the shed, but Irene kept the Vauxhall up by the building. A smart move, in Joe's opinion, as the grass was still quite soggy.

The coroner and his assistant stood off to the side, waiting. Miss Flaversham was with them, wrapped up in a shawl and stifling a yawn. They all straightened as the pair approached them.

From beside the shed, Lestrade threw his long arms out in an annoyed gesture.

"Irene, no one is telling me anything. They all insist I wait for you. What is going on and why did you need *me* to drive all the way here? Also, can we please get that body moved now? I've made my observations."

"Yes. The body can be taken."

The DI waved at the two gentlemen to get a stretcher. He then turned back for an explanation, which Irene happily started into.

"Two students have run away. The one girl, Lizzie, has apparently left with a nice fellow she met in town. The other girl, Charlotte, is a bit more complicated. Two men were visiting her at night and at first, we thought it was the victim, Tobias Clarke III, who had taken her. It turns out she has actually left with a Spanish man whom we suspect she loves, and one of them may have murdered this boy here."

Lestrade pinched the bridge of his nose. "Do we know where Charlotte is now?"

Irene hesitated. "We are not sure, but we think she may be returning to her home tonight. What we need you to do, though, is wait until we find her before informing this man's parents of his death."

"What? Take him to the morgue in London and ring them up tomorrow? No, Irene."

She stepped closer to her childhood friend. Perhaps out of intimidation or desperation, Joe didn't know, but it had no effect on Lestrade. "Please Eddy. If we inform them of his death, they may go straight over to the Bancroft estate and cause a scene. Then, Charlotte may never return home."

"I know what you are asking, and I understand why, but I'm sorry. I've done a lot for you, but holding back information about the death of a child from his parents is something I will not do. Especially since he's been dead for so long."

"Eddy."

"No."

Joe winced and prepared for Irene's retaliation. He was also ready to jump in. As much as he wanted to solve this case, he agreed with Lestrade in this particular instance. He placed a hand gently on his partner's shoulder. At first, she was tense under his grip, but quickly relaxed.

Irene finally nodded. "Fine. I understand. But will you at least keep details of our case quiet? They already know that Charlotte has gone missing, and that their son was a suspect. We are close to solving this, Eddy."

He sighed. "I will do what I can, but with Scotland Yard involved now, there are certain procedures I must adhere to."

"Adhere to them, but hold them off as long as you can."

"And when you find this girl, am I allowed to arrest her for murder?"

"Um…"

"Irene!"

"Tobias was not a nice boy," she thrust her hand at the coroners packing the body into the car. "It's been stated that he's made unwanted passes at women. Obviously, he was in this shed to do *something* to Charlotte. If this was out of self-defence, then I cannot abide a murder charge."

Lestrade sucked in an impatient breath and scrubbed a hand over his face. When he spoke next, his words were calm but commanding. "Here's what will happen: I will get a statement from both of you to type into a report and rule you both out as suspects. I will then take the body and contact the family, letting them know that we've now partnered with you, that Charlotte is still missing and we have no idea of her whereabouts—"

"Make it known that she is *not* at her house."

"Irene."

"Please."

"Fine. I will strongly suggest that she has fled, but we have a good idea of her whereabouts. I will advise the parents not to travel anywhere. You must promise to inform me when you find her. If she *did* kill this man, you know I'll work hard to make sure there is a fair investigation and trial, should it come to that."

Irene chewed her lip. She looked ready with a plan of her own.

Joe held a soft grip on her shoulder, drumming his fingers against her jacket.

She blew sharply out of her nose and folded her arms across her chest. "That is satisfactory."

Lestrade huffed a tired laugh. "Well, I should hope so."

Irene tossed her head. Joe couldn't help but smile at his friend's stubbornness.

"Doctor, you must show me that trick," Lestrade said. "It's as if you pushed a button that calmed her instantly."

Joe laughed despite himself and wrapped his arm around his friend's shoulder. "I risk getting my fingers bit every time I do that, but it works on most occasions."

Irene scowled at the two men. "Let's get these statements over with. We have lots to do and very little time to do them."

* * * * *

A few hours later, in the pitch dark, Joe and Irene sat behind a rather large pine tree at the edge of the Bancroft estate. The almost-full moon was on their side tonight, lighting up the back lawn and the rear of the house.

Irene peered through a pair of binoculars, then let out a sigh in the quiet of the night. She dug through her bag, producing two bread rolls they'd taken from the hotel and handing one to Joe.

She was getting restless, which was unusual for her during this type of work. He'd seen her sit for hours and wait for a resolution.

"I have an odd thought." He attempted to occupy her mind, "Do you think we would've been friends when we were younger?"

"I didn't have friends." Irene's gaze was locked on the house. "Well, I had Eddy, but he doesn't count."

"If we had met as teenagers, do you think we would've struck up a friendship?"

"We are friends now, aren't we?"

"Yes, but I was much different as a boy. I was shy. I didn't speak to anyone. My sisters did all the talking."

She sat back against the trunk of a tree. "Then, I don't suspect so. I didn't speak to anyone either unless I was forced to or I was looking to gain information for one of my father's cases, or the small cases that I pursued on my own."

Joe shifted on the blanket, trying to avoid the root he kept sitting on. "Imagine if we had met?"

"What do you mean?"

"I took many trips to London with my father. It would be a funny tale if we had crossed paths beforehand. I guess we have no way of knowing."

"Yes, we do. We'll go over the timeline of your trips and cross reference them with where I was in the city. It would be a fun weekend project."

"Perhaps when we have a weekend free."

Irene smirked at him as the moonlight caught her big, dark eyes. "You are humouring me, but I warn you to tread lightly, because I will hold you to that plan."

* * * * *

Two hours later, at nearly 3am, Joe peered through the binoculars once more. All the lights were off in the estate excluding one, but the moon still gave enough light that they could see if anyone approached.

He had offered to keep watch if Irene wanted to grab an hour of sleep, but she refused. Instead, she'd gone into her observing pose – cross-legged, fingers steepled and pressed to her lips, gaze unwavering. Joe wasn't even sure of the last time she blinked.

After what seemed an eternity, she finally spoke. "I have been thinking."

He set the binoculars down. "When are you not?"

She continued, ignoring his jibe at her. "Why do people call Spanish the language of love? I've heard that expression before, but do not understand it."

"Because of the way it sounds, I suppose. It's melodic. Musical even. I feel like any language where they roll their r's sounds lovely. Of course, I haven't heard enough Spanish all at once to be certain."

His friend pursed her lips and nodded at some decision she must've come to. "I think I shall delve deeper into different languages over the summer."

"With your brain, you could certainly pick up one or two. I learned German fast enough."

She looked at him with a fierce expression in her eyes. "You were forced to learn it, my dear Joe, if only to survive. Hopefully, it does not come to that for me. I shall find a tutor."

He chuckled at her concern. "A much better idea. Also, learning a language is a far better use of your time than cross-referencing if we'd met as youngsters."

"Oh, a new language wouldn't deter me from that. Plus, that project would only take an afternoon or—"

Suddenly, like a dog seeing a mouse to chase, Irene spotted something in the field and was on her feet in an instant.

Chapter VII

A Tale of Star-Crossed Lovers

Charlotte sprinted across the lawn toward the house, dress fluttering behind her. She reached the building, stopping at the last window on the lower floor. After a quick glance around, the girl opened the pane and slipped inside.

Irene grabbed Joe's hand. "Come on. Rosa's brother must be somewhere in those trees."

She took off, dragging him along. As they hurried through the woods, she released his hand, finding it much easier to scurry amongst the trees without impediment. The night wind whistled as she ran on her toes, tapping the ground lightly with each step.

Soon, they were on the other side of the forest. Irene slowed, crouching slightly to sneak up quietly on the man sat there, waiting for his lover. It took a moment to find him in the dark, but she spotted him right on the edge of the treeline.

Rosa's brother peered out, clinging to a tree with his shoulders bunched. He was nervous, worried that Charlotte may not come back to him.

Behind Irene, Joe stepped on a branch, snapping in the air like a firework. The man whirled around on his heel and cussed in Spanish. Even though he was backlit against the moonlight, his black hair flowed in the wind, and his stature was ready to fight.

Irene held up her hands. "Easy, *senor*. We're not the police. We are here to talk."

She could just make out a face in the dark; his light eyes were big and scared. The man turned to Joe, inching back, but still poised for a fight.

She spoke to him again. "My name is Irene Holmes. This is my friend, Doctor Watson. We are private investigators, but we are on your side. What's your name?"

Rosa's brother glanced behind him at the estate, then back to them. "*¿Mi nombre?* It's Carlos. We did nothing... Ah, Charlotte did nothing wrong. We want to leave."

His accent was thicker than his sister's, but his words were sincere. The boy was nervous, prone to flee like a frightened rabbit. He leaned to the one side ever so slightly, favouring an injury on his torso.

"You have not done 'nothing' Carlos," Irene said. "You've left a dead body in your wake."

It took him a second to process her comment, then he shook his head feverishly. "Charlotte did not kill him."

A clear lie. Irene was curious to what extent it would go. How much was he willing to cover up for his beloved?

"You're lying."

He shook his head again, mop of hair bouncing with the movement. "No. No lie. She did not kill him. He was angry and said very bad things to her. We started to fight. He stabbed me. I pushed him and he fell."

Carlos wrapped his arms around himself, glancing back at the house.

There was no sign of Charlotte returning yet, and luckily for them, this young man seemed determined to wait for her.

He did love her, at least as far as Irene could tell. She'd have to find a way to ask Joe if he thought the same; he was better with emotions than she was.

In the moment, she pressed on with her questioning. They had him cornered, so she might as well gather all the information she could before they took off again – or Eddy showed up and arrested him.

Irene still wasn't sure which way she wanted this case to go. Right now, it was in her hands whether she let the young couple escape or keep them for an arrest.

"The evidence suggests otherwise. He did not fall and hit his head."

Carlos jabbed his fingers into his chest. "*I* did it. I pushed him."

Irene sighed and folded her arms. "While you were being stabbed, someone hit him in the back of the head with a rock. Then you both made it look like he slipped and fell."

He went silent, head hung. She wanted to bombard him with more questions but suspected that he may shut down or retaliate.

Joe stepped forward then, speaking in the friendly tone that was needed when Irene was about to push an interrogation.

"Why did he meet you in the shed? Was it to stop you, or did he have some other plan in mind?"

Carlos opened his mouth, then shut it. He dropped his hands to his side for a brief moment before running his fingers through his hair, causing the strands to fluff up.

When he spoke, his words were defeated and tired. "I was waiting for Charlotte in the shed. She came in upset. He followed her in. He was there for her. To take her away with him. Said his parents would kill him if he didn't marry her. He was drunk and very angry. I did not know what he meant, but Charlotte did. She was crying. She called him some very bad names that I was surprised to hear fall from her mouth. He went after her, but I fought him away. Please do not get her in trouble."

"We haven't yet," Irene cut in. "We are inclined to help you both."

Carlos perked up. "Help us?"

Joe held up his hand, shooting a glance at his partner.

"Inclined to help. We must know more, though."

Irene looked back at him, barely making out his worried expression in the dark. He assumed she'd let Carlos and Charlotte go, even though they'd killed a man. But she needed more information. Since she had pulled in Eddy to help with the investigation, she couldn't let the couple simply walk away.

But she could sway the narrative.

"Were you part of your sister's plan to get Charlotte's money by marriage and then by poison?"

Carlos swallowed hard, then crouched to the ground, locking his fingers behind his neck.

"I am shamed to say yes," he muttered, forcing Irene and Joe to take a step forward to hear him. "I was to marry her and then I would get her family's money as revenge for my sister being treated so bad. But..."

"You fell in love," Joe offered.

"I was not supposed to. She was to fall in love with me. But I got it backwards."

Joe let out a soft laugh. "That's usually how it happens."

Irene looked between the two men as annoyance nipped at her. "It was love that really made you abandon your sister and her plan?"

The boy stood up. "I did not like the plan from the start. But, yes. Charlotte… *es perfecta*."

The way he spoke about his love gave Irene pause. There was

no doubt the man was entirely taken with the girl, but she didn't understand why they took such risks to be together. She needed to cease thinking about the consequences of love and focus back on this case or else she'd be there for hours.

She peered around Carlos to the estate.

"Charlotte is taking quite a while. What was she retrieving?"

"Food, clothes, items she had put away."

"How long have you both been speaking about running away?"

"It was before Christmas. I met her in town. It only took me a few times of visiting her to know that I was in love and wanted nothing to do with my sister's plan."

An additional worry settled over Irene. If Charlotte had everything prepared, then why was she spending so much time inside the house?

"Where have you been staying since you left the doctor?" Joe asked, still in interview mode.

"Charlotte has a house in those trees, from when she was a child. We stayed there so I could rest during the day and heal."

That weighted blanket of shame cloaked Irene again. How could she have been so stupid as to not search the property or ask if Charlotte had some place she liked to hide in?

And what was taking her so long now?

"She should've returned by now."

Carlos spun around to the house. "Is she in danger?"

"I don't know."

The boy moved forward, but Irene grabbed his sleeve.

"You stay right here. I will locate her."

"I can—"

"No." She tightened her grip. "While I believe your story, I do not fully trust you not to flee, if only to escape and come back for Charlotte. I will go. Please do not run. Doctor Watson may not look it, but he has the skills to detain you."

Carlos glanced warily at Joe. "*Si.*"

Irene secured her bag tighter and grabbed the binoculars, then took off. Pausing briefly at the treeline, she scoured the windows for anyone on the lookout, but could see no one.

Of course, the moment she ran across the bit of back lawn to the side of the house, her presence would be obvious to anyone even glancing out, but she had to take that chance.

Running as fast as her feet would carry her, heels patting the soft grass, Irene made it right to the house and pressed against the cool brick wall. She allowed herself a moment to catch her breath before sneaking down the side. The barn on the far left had been converted to store automobiles. She could see one of the stable-turned-car boys mulling about the flat above. His second-story room was the only light source on this side of the house.

Her plan was to peer inside the windows as sneakily as possible, but a sound from the front of the house captured her attention. Gravel crunched from far in the distance as a car approached.

Irene hastened to the front and looked around the wall.

It hurried up the road, headlights bouncing as it spit rocks and dust. Irene muttered a curse.

The Clarkes' automobile.

And judging by their driving, they were not happy.

How the hell did they know to come here? Surely, Eddy wouldn't have called them as Irene specifically told him not to.

Regardless, he needed to get here quick. Before all hell broke loose.

She turned back to the automobile garage, aiming for the small flat above. She vaulted over the half door and pulled herself quickly up the ladder. The poor boy gave a cry of surprise, almost knocking over a table.

"Is there a telephone up here?" Irene said, frantic.

He nodded.

"Excellent. Phone DI Lestrade at the Lakefront Hotel in town and get him here at once. Do you understand?"

The boy nodded again, but didn't move.

"Do it now!"

This time, he obeyed.

Irene dropped back out into the night. From the screech of tires, the car had come to a stop. She froze in her tracks, debating where to go.

A brief shriek and a slamming door gave her the answer.

She pivoted, aiming for the back lawn.

Charlotte tore off across the grass, a bundle of items in her arms. Rosa appeared not a second later, pursuing the young woman.

Irene muttered another curse. She ran down the treeline, parallel to the two girls. Tree bark scratched her skin and she almost fell twice, but she kept up with the girls as they sprinted.

She followed the trees as they curved around to where Joe and Carlos waited. The boy rushed out, embracing his lover in the moonlit field.

Rosa caught up to them, rage in her eyes.

Irene launched herself at the woman. The two collapsed on the ground, rolling a few times. She did one more somersault and stood up. Her head whirled, heart thrumming in her ears. But she spun around, ready for Rosa's attack.

Chapter VIII

An Exchange of Bullets

Carlos and Charlotte clung to one another as they shuffled away from the action. Joe immediately placed himself between Rosa and his friend, giving her a moment to catch her breath.

The maid got to her feet and spun to her brother. She started yelling in Spanish and Irene stepped out to intervene.

Rosa didn't advance, though. She just yelled.

Carlos shouted back. They locked themselves in an argument in a flowing, flowery language.

Charlotte hid behind her beloved while Joe attempted to protect Irene. They needed to stop the shouting before more people exited the house.

"Everyone, silence," Irene bellowed, but they didn't stop. She finally wedged herself between the arguing siblings. "Enough. Both of you shut up."

Rosa snarled something in Spanish, but stepped back and folded her arms across her chest. Carlos kept a protective hand on Charlotte but pursed his lips.

Joe placed himself within striking distance of the young man, should he become an issue.

With everyone cooperating, Irene turned to Rosa. "Your plan has failed. The best thing for you to do is keep silent."

Charlotte piped up from behind Carlos. "What plan? Rosa, what's going on?"

The other girl didn't offer an answer, so Irene provided one. "To let you both elope, then to kill your parents so you inherit the money. This would make you both rich. I suspect Carlos would have given some money to Rosa. I am, however, still trying to determine if she would've actually killed you, Charlotte."

The girl let out a small gasp, stepping away. Even in the darkness, Joe saw tears well in her eyes and felt an immense pity for the poor girl.

Carlos moved forward, but Joe grabbed his arm. Thankfully, he didn't resist. The boy stumbled over his words, attempting to explain.

"Charlotte, *mi amor*. I–"

She cut him off, though. "This was all *fake*? I don't... I can't..."

Carlos spoke to her in Spanish, repeating the words '*te amo*' over and over. Charlotte just kept shaking her head and looking at the ground in disbelief. In the background, Rosa fumed, waiting for her brother to be done pleading.

To Joe's surprise, Irene offered the young woman comfort. "He does love you, Charlotte. He was in the midst of betraying his own sister for you. However, everything is now a mess, and we all must wait for DI Lestrade to arrive."

"A detective," Charlotte gasped. "But all I did was enter my own home! We did nothing wrong."

Carlos lowered his head and spoke to her. "They found Tobias."

The girl's eyes widened. She looked between Joe and Irene frantically.

Rosa, who'd been tensed and ready for a fight the entire time, softened ever so slightly. "Tobias?"

"He is dead."

A small smile fell across her face. In the dark of the night, she looked like a villain in a storybook, sending a shiver down Joe's spine.

"Everything will be laid out and dealt with once the detective inspector gets here," Irene said. "He'll want to speak with all of you."

Rosa interjected. "I am not waiting for police. I did nothing wrong."

"I believe criminal conspiracy still counts. And as for you, Charlotte, no matter how well you staged that crime scene, there was evidence that you hit Tobias over the head."

"We had no choice," the girl cried. "He was there that night I left. It was just a bad coincidence. I made the mistake of telling him I was in love with someone else. He wouldn't leave me alone. I tried to get rid of him, but he came right to the shed with me. He was going to kill Carlos!"

A slamming door came from behind them. Cries of shock and surprise followed.

Joe turned to look across the field and cussed a thousand times in his head. The Bancrofts and the Clarkes rushed toward them. Mr. Bancroft had a rifle in his hands, charging like an angry bull.

Joe stepped forward, putting himself between Irene as the mob of angry parents crossed the lawn.

"Charlotte!" Mrs. Bancroft called as they approached. "What on *earth* are you doing?"

Luckily, they stopped a good distance from the group. Mr. Bancroft kept the rifle down, but the weapon still made Joe uneasy.

The man thrust a finger at Carlos. "What have you done to my little girl?"

Joe raised his hands to stop the shouting, but Mrs. Clarke called over him to Charlotte. "You killed my son, you harlot!"

Mr. Bancroft pivoted to the woman. "What did you call her?"

Mr. Clarke jumped in, "Don't you yell at her!"

"Enough!" Irene shouted, louder than Joe had ever heard. "For god's sake, you are all worse than children! Put that gun away, Mr. Bancroft, before you shoot yourself in the eye. Tobias is dead, yes. He attacked Charlotte and was killed out of self-defence."

Mrs. Clarke let out a gurgled, angry scream and spat at Charlotte. "He loved you, you bitch!"

Joe stepped forward. The four enraged parents were enough to make him want to put a full suit of armour on Irene, lest they all decide to attack.

His partner kept at them, though, obviously angry at them all. "He confessed before he attacked her that he never loved her and was simply marrying her for her money – at his parents' urging, we should note." She spat the rest of her words. "All of you put this poor girl through hell. And for what? Money? You all were willing to lie and cheat and kill, regardless of how it would affect a family. You both came up with the same sickening plan and all of you should be locked away for such irresponsible and evil thoughts."

Rosa stepped forward and thrust a finger at the Bancrofts. "It is *them* who should be in jail. They tossed my family aside like we were nothing when the war came. We could not even go back to our own country. We could not find jobs anywhere because we were *filthy Spaniards*." She rounded on the Clarke's next. "And your son was a disgusting pig. The things he would say to Charlotte and I. He should have been dead long ago."

Mr. Bancroft spun to Mr. Clarke. "Your son did *what* to my daughter?"

"He did nothing of the sort," the other man spat back. "He was a good boy."

"He hardly seems like one!" Despite the gun on his back, Mr. Bancroft took a swing.

To Clarke's credit, he sidestepped. Bancroft stumbled forward and the rifle dropped to the ground. The man then turned and attacked Clarke again.

Joe kept his eye on the gun. If he could get to it, he'd have enough authority to silence the entire group and force them to co-operate until Lestrade arrived. He was also tempted to tell Irene to take Charlotte and Carlos and run from the scene.

The two fathers swung at each other like children while their wives yelled.

Joe looked at Irene, but her focus was on the rifle. She probably had the same idea, but she had to cross the gauntlet to get to it. It was up to him.

As he advanced, though, Rosa let out a loud, angry scream. She launched herself toward the gun. Joe froze as the maid jumped back, away from the crowd, swinging the rifle up. She aimed the barrel from the Bancrofts to Charlotte.

Irene stepped in line of the gunfire, blocking Rosa's shot.

Joe's heart dropped into his stomach and he sucked in a sharp breath. He tried to tell her to move, but no words came out.

She was still a few metres away. There was a slight chance the shot would miss, but there was a greater chance that bullet would rip right through Irene.

His mouth went dry and his stomach churned over and over, like a heavy lump of butter.

The four parents gasped in union, but remained still.

"I will not go to jail," Rosa cried. "And I will not have the world think that your son was a good man. All I want is the money to leave and give my parents the life they deserve. Because none of you deserve what you have."

"We gave you everything," Mrs. Bancroft shouted, though her voice wavered as she stared at the gun. "We let you play with our daughter as if she was your sister."

"And then you threw us out." Rosa tilted her head onto the rifle, aiming.

Irene shuffled sideways.

"Rosa," she said, voice even and cool. "Put the rifle down. You do not need to add murder to your list of crimes."

But the maid didn't budge. Her jaw muscle twitched in the moonlight. She was about to pull the trigger.

Instinct propelled him forward.

Joe dived into Irene. He knocked her aside as a gunshot cracked the air. Sharp, hot pain seared just below his ribs as he dropped on the soft grass.

Despite the pain, he kept his eyes on Irene.

She'd stumbled sideways, free from harm. Joe sighed in relief, the pain still shooting through him.

Then she pulled her uncle's revolver.

She aimed it at the furious Spanish girl.

Rosa saw the gun in her hand and spun, ready to fire again.

Joe cried out and tried to move forward to protect Irene again.

But she was faster.

The revolver went off, deafening Joe for a second.

Rosa shrieked in pain, collapsing on the ground.

Joe stayed on his knees, prepared to help Irene if needed. But tears filled his eyes and panic replaced the adrenaline rushing through his body.

Rosa wailed as blood oozed through her fingers. From behind Joe, Carlos rushed forward, but Irene swung at him.

"Everyone into the field and on your knees."

Carlos and Charlotte shuffled around to stand with the parents. They all took a few steps away from Rosa before getting on their knees.

Irene moved beside Joe and he sighed with relief. She was safe. The danger was over. Sinking fully to the ground eased the pain of the bullet wound ever so slightly.

Sirens sounded from the distance and the flashing lights of the police tore across the back lawn.

Joe leaned on Irene's leg for support as a fresh wave of pain hit him.

"Hang on, Joe." The faintest of tremors snaked through her voice.

"I'm fine. It just hurts."

He leaned on her more and felt her hand curl gently into his hair. The tears in his eyes almost fell, but he blinked them back, staying strong until Lestrade arrived.

The DI's Wolseley parked behind the group and the man leapt out immediately. Four other constables went straight to the six people sitting on the ground and the pair of parents all started shouting about solicitors.

Carlos and Charlotte stayed silent.

Lestrade scooped up the rifle, slinging it over his shoulder, as an ambulance trundled across the lawn. He shouted at the newly arrived paramedics before crouching at Rosa. She whimpered softly, curled into a ball.

With the rifle secured, Irene dropped to her knees beside Joe. He instinctively held his hand up, letting her know that he was okay. He tried to tell her as much, but couldn't speak. Panic gripped at his lungs as the pain continued into his ribs.

He sunk lower to the ground.

Irene grabbed at his shirt, trying to see the wound.

"I am fine, Irene. It's just—"

His sentence was cut off by a wince of pain.

"There is so much blood," she said. "Stay still so I can put pressure on it."

He wiggled away from her hand.

"Stay still, dammit," she snapped, her voice cracking in the middle of her words.

Joe steeled himself, her worry and panic scaring him. Her eyes were enormous as she frantically searched for the wound.

He lay back on the grass, head woozy, but his anxiety eased.

Lestrade appeared above him. "You got yourself shot, Doctor."

Joe chuckled despite himself. "I certainly did."

Irene was not in a joking mood at all. She rounded on the poor DI. "Where is the damn ambulance?"

He crouched to see Joe's wound. "They're tending to the woman with the life-threatening injuries first."

"This could be life-threatening!"

"Irene," Joe breathed. "Pressure on the wound, not on my lungs."

She cussed and eased up, refusing to look at him.

Heavy footsteps came to them and two medics crouched at Joe.

Lestrade took Irene's arm, but she fought him.

"Let them work," he said. "You need to tell me who I'm arresting."

But Irene didn't move.

Joe sat up as best he could and touched her shoulder. "I'm fine, Irene. Go finish this case."

She stepped away then and Joe finally let out a ragged, long breath. Tears welled in his eyes again and he laid back down in the grass as the medics took over.

Chapter IX

A Talk of Bologna and Bees

Irene hesitated, stalling until the last second. Joe's wound wasn't life-threatening, but she couldn't leave him while she dealt with silly rich people's problems. She curled her fingers into fists to stop a tremor as she tried to see around the medic, but Eddy gently steered her away.

Once she was a safe distance, he spoke to her. "What happened? Who am I arresting?"

Irene took one final glance at Joe before releasing a long sigh.

She explained the two plans to woo Charlotte so she and her husband would receive an inheritance. How Rosa had planned to poison the Bancrofts to ensure her brother received the money.

"She is the one you should arrest. I would've given her a pass, but she shot Joe. I have extra handcuffs if you need them."

She looked at the two paramedics working on Rosa, trying to

get her on a gurney.

"You shot her in the gut," Eddy said. "She may not even make it to the hospital."

"Oh. Well, then we have nothing to worry about."

"This got messy, Irene. You'll need to make several statements. I know you want to get back to Joe, but—"

Irene peered around him at Charlotte and Carlos. Despite the cuffs keeping their hands behind their backs, they leaned on one another for comfort.

For the briefest of moments, Irene was on their side, rooting for them. They tried to escape to make their own future.

"Will they be separated for long?"

Eddy followed her gaze. "I honestly don't know. I am surprised you're so invested in young love."

"I'm not opposed to love. It just makes people do foolish things sometimes."

The DI bumped her shoulder and nodded to Joe behind them. "Like take a bullet?"

She turned to see the paramedic trying to talk him into letting them bring a gurney out for him as well.

Irene snorted. "That is loyalty and idiocy."

"Uh, huh." Eddy gave her a soft, brotherly smile, then flicked a rogue curl from her face. "I have to gather my prisoners. I'll meet you both at the hospital."

Irene took a moment to calm her racing heart. They'd finally got Rosa on a gurney and wheeled her to the ambulance. The four parents were still shouting over one another, but the constables were walking them away from the scene. Charlotte and Carlos were being loaded into the back of a police car.

And a paramedic was helping Joe get on his feet.

The headlights from the ambulance and police cars lit up the field, casting an eery shadow on the large estate behind.

This case got messy, and it wasn't even over. She still needed to contact Miss Flaversham and inform her of Charlotte's return. She also still needed find out exactly what happened to Lizzie and if she was safe.

A yawn overtook her as she started back to her dear friend.

* * * * *

The early hours of the morning were full of activity. Everyone was being carted to the small police outpost. They whisked Rosa away to the hospital, along with Joe, much to his chagrin.

Irene followed in the Vauxhall, yawning all the way.

She sat in the hallway outside the room where they were stitching him up. The bright lights made her close her eyes and she almost nodded off. Her feet hurt, so she kicked off her boots and untucked her blouse. A rogue hairpin had fallen to the floor earlier as well, but she couldn't be bothered to pick it up.

Sharp heels sounded from the distance. Miss Flaversham

turned the corner.

"Miss Holmes." Her voice was tired, as if she had been up all night too.

Irene didn't straighten her posture or even attempt anything other than a curt nod.

"I am terribly sorry about everything," the headmistress started. "For all the trouble you've been through."

Irene noted the slight remorse in her voice. "You called the Clarkes, didn't you?"

Miss Flaversham stared at the floor. "I thought it was the proper thing to do. Their son was dead after all—"

"I told you not to." Irene straightened, ready for a confrontation.

"I know. This mistake was completely on me, and I am truly sorry."

She wanted to argue with the elegant, foolish woman; to point out how her actions affected this entire night, and to scream at her for getting Joe shot.

Her body, though, was simply too tired to do anything more than shake her head. "Nothing can change what transpired tonight. Your guilt should be punishment enough for not listening to simple instructions. We'll keep you apprised about Lizzie's fate, but otherwise, we are done. Should there be a bill for Doctor Watson's care, I will send it to you to cover. Good day."

For a moment, Irene thought Miss Flaversham might retort, as the stunned look on her face was masking her inner narrative. Instead, the woman gave a small curtsey and left.

* * * * *

Joe wasn't in hospital for very long – just enough to receive half a dozen stitches, a bandage to be changed every twelve hours for a few days, and a prescription of medicine. The bullet had grazed him but had done minor damage. Irene had already picked up their overnight bags from the hotel and soon they were on their way back to Baker Street, the sunrise guiding their drive.

Miss Hudson fussed over them and brought them copious amounts of tea after they'd arrived. By mid-morning, they sat in their respective chairs – Irene by the fire and Joe next to her.

She had just tugged a blanket over her to catch a nap when the telephone rang sharp and loud. She trudged over to the small table beside the door. "Irene Holmes speaking"

"Good morning," Eddy's voice chirped. "Or is it almost noon? I have no idea. I wanted to see how your knight-in-shining-armour was doing?"

She peered at Joe under a blanket, eyes half-closed. "He is fine. Tired and sore, but he'll live."

"Wonderful. Would you like the hearty conclusion to this

convoluted case?"

"I would. Then I would suggest you have a glass of water and not to touch coffee for the rest of the day."

"Deal." He laughed, then let out a long-suffering sigh. "Rosa survived, but will remain in hospital until she is well enough to travel, then will be sent back to Spain. What she does after that is up to her. Carlos has no crimes against him. Charlotte has claimed self-defence. The whole thing may not even go to court because, as rumour has it, the Bancrofts are going to pay a hell of a sum to the Clarkes to banish the entire trial."

"Can they do that?"

"People with money can do anything," Eddy said, the tiredness now creeping into his voice. "As for Lizzie, that case is closed as well. She met someone on her travels and eloped. Her mother received a letter just yesterday from her. They've apparently settled somewhere north of London. Finally, a young woman from the school named Annette sent a letter to the police station for you. She says if you ever need help, she is more than willing."

Irene mirrored his sigh. "Well, that all seems grand."

"It does. Now, go tend to the patient and get some sleep."

"Thank you, Eddy. Goodbye."

Irene leaned on the table for a moment. The case was closed, and she was exhausted. Her mistake still hung on her. It was as if she'd gone back in time to when she was truly an amateur.

Perhaps she simply needed more cases to practice.

Or maybe she was losing her touch.

Her stomach turned at that last thought.

Dispelling it from her mind, Irene headed to her chair. Joe stirred as she passed, eyeing his cup of tea on the table. He winced as he leaned forward, swiping the mug. She watched, ready to jump in, but he was faster than she anticipated. Soon he sat back, sipping at the beverage.

"What a production. I feel like I could sleep for ten years."

"That would be the morphine they gave you. Of which I will put away should you not use it all."

"For the next time one of us is shot?"

The pair laughed, but a question weighed on Irene's mind that hearkened back to Eddy's words at the Bancroft estate. Something made her hesitate, which she rarely did, as most questions formed in her head demanded to be answered. This, however, felt like it was from her heart, not her head. The answer would come with feelings rather than facts.

She looked at her friend who had a loopy grin on his face. "Would you take a bullet for Sarah?"

Joe focused on her, narrowing his eyes. "Um, I don't know—"

"Or Eddy?" Her heart rate sped up, her palms clammy. She should've kept the question to herself.

It was obvious – Joe would most certainly jump in front of a gun for Sarah or Eddy.

Right?

She opened her mouth to tell him to forget everything, but Joe beat her to it.

"Perhaps?" He ran a hand through his already messy hair. "I honestly wasn't even thinking about it, Irene. I saw the gun pointed at you and I acted on instinct."

"I don't think Eddy would take a bullet for me." As soon as the words left her mouth, she knew they weren't true.

"Irene. You're loved more than you think. And I know you know this."

"Yes," she scoffed. "I do know this, and it makes me uneasy."

Joe laughed. "Love makes you uneasy?"

"I do not want to be a burden. I don't need people doing foolish things on my behalf. Whether out of love, loyalty, or fear. Well, out of fear may not be that bad."

"You want to be respected," he corrected. "Not feared."

"Yes, I suppose that's what it is."

"And you do want to be loved." His voice drifted off, the morphine grabbing him again.

She squirmed and pulled her knees up to her chest.

"I'm sure many young men fell for you when you were younger," he teased. "Oh, heck, I've seen men fall for you since *I've* known you."

"I don't remember men falling for me or tripping over themselves to ask me to go dancing."

"Baloney. I bet they did."

"Well, even if they did, I would've knocked them out."

"Who knows, maybe *I* would've been completely smitten with young Irene."

"And who's to say I wouldn't have knocked you out as well?"

Joe clutched his chest. "Oh, to have such an honour."

Irene guffawed and tossed a pillow at him. It smacked him square in the face.

His eyes went wide with the surprise. He leaned over to grab the cushion from the floor, then winced.

"Also," he said, voice clear again. "I'm about to keep you uneasy."

"What do you mean?"

"I asked Miss Hudson about your father's bees."

"Oh?" Irene's heart sped up again. She hugged her knees tighter. She was surprised that a small part of her was genuinely curious. That feeling almost overtook the hesitance that usually sprung up whenever speaking about her father's life on his farm.

"Out of his five hives, only two survived the winter."

Her voice cracked with sadness when she spoke. "Only two?"

"Irene and Ginny."

"Who are Irene and Ginny?"

Joe hesitated, then gulped at his tea. "I thought you knew about the queens. Apparently, your uncle told your father to name the queens of each hive after someone he holds dear in hopes it would help his memory."

Irene's eyebrows pulled together. She couldn't recall Uncle John ever saying this. But, of course, she had moved back to London as he was setting up a few new hives.

Why wouldn't Miss Hudson have told her this, then?

Her face grew hot as she remembered all the times she'd silenced the landlady for speaking about her father.

"Who is Ginny?" She asked, shifting the focus from her feelings.

Joe laughed. "Miss Hudson's name is Virginia."

"Oh. I knew that."

"Baloney again."

"Stop saying baloney!"

Irene felt a bit of guilt for not knowing Miss Hudson's name, and even more unease at the fact that she never knew Father named his queens. What did he name the others? Was this Queen Irene the first of her kind? Or had there been others? Was she doing well? How was her hive? What hive number was she? Hive six was notorious for defensive bees, but was that her hive or Ginny's? Had Hive Six even survived the winter?

She thought about asking Joe all of this, but knew he'd have no answer. Miss Hudson was the person to ask, but that held the risk of falling into a trap as the older woman told her story after story until Irene got rude and silenced her.

Joe must've been feeling very relaxed, because he suddenly

spoke so easily and without hesitation, when normally he would shift about and stall until Irene called him out.

"You never got around to writing that letter to your father. Now would be a great time."

She instantly deflected. "Right now? While both of us are overtired, one of us is high, and the other wishes she was?"

He crumpled up a napkin and tossed it at her. "When we are both well. We can sit down and write it together. Or you may write it on your own and I can read it after. Or you may write it and never show me."

"Or I may never write it at all."

"Irene." Joe straightened to command authority, but his head wobbled and his auburn hair stuck up in the back from slouching in the chair. "You will write a letter. Even if you don't send it. By god, you will write one."

As funny as his commanding voice was, he was serious. He was trying to help her. A sensation like a crowd of butterflies stirred in her stomach. Joe was so committed to helping her that he looked downright clownish as he tried to focus on her face.

Irene's cheeks warmed as the butterflies flapped about. She rolled her shoulders back to rid her body of the heat.

"Fine, when we are both rested, I will attempt a letter."

"Jolly good!" Joe lifted his mug and took a sip, pulling the cup in but frowning. "Oh. I'm out."

Irene stood. "Let me get you another."

"No. The lavatory is so far away."

She giggled at his lament, a silly, girly sound. Then she cleared her throat.

"If you have to go, I can help you to the toilet, but once you are inside, you are on your own."

He held the dish out for her. "Then more tea it is!"

She took it, then saw the saucer sitting on the table. "I wonder…"

Irene set the mug on the saucer, then perched the lot on the top of her head. She only adjusted it once before letting her hands fall gently to her side. Tucking one foot behind the other, she lowered her body in a perfect curtsy.

The mug and saucer stayed perfectly balanced, and she let out a victorious cry. "See, Joe. I'm just as good as those women in the school."

Her friend laughed, the sound loose and happy because of the medication. "Marvellous! Simply marvellous! Next stop, dinner with the Queen!"

In all the excitement, Isla jumped up from her spot on the couch and barked. Irene startled, then let out a panicked cry as the cup and saucer slid sideways. She danced around like a madwoman trying to balance it, but it was too late.

The saucer smashed against the wooden table, breaking into a dozen pieces. The cup followed, snapping in two on the ground.

Within a second, their landlady's angry voice shouted from the bottom of the stairs. "What are you two doing?"

"Nothing, Miss Hudson," Irene said as Joe giggled from beside her. "Everything is fine."

They both waited, but the woman stayed downstairs. Irene looked at Joe as they burst out in laughter.

"Do not tell her how this broke." She warned, grinning ear to ear.

He put his hand to his heart. "Your secret is safe with me. Though the more medicine I take, the more I might mistake you for one another."

She smacked him on the shoulder. "Joe Watson, that is *not* funny!"

"I am kidding," he said, rolling his arm and grimacing. "I could never mistake you for anyone else in the entire world, Irene Holmes."

"I should think not."

Joe then gave her the smile that occasionally cropped up on his face. A gentle expression, his eyebrows relaxed, as if remembering some fond memory.

Those damn butterflies made their way back into Irene's stomach.

She busied herself by crouching to pick up the broken pieces.

Still, a smile crept across her own lips as she thought about how soft and sweet Joe was being, and how he had, without thinking of himself, jumped in front of a bullet for her.

She didn't dwell on those thoughts for long, or the implication of butterflies in her belly, because Isla scurried over to her. The dog attempted to lick her face as she tidied up. Joe laughed from his chair, calling the dog away, but she didn't listen. Irene was on the floor, which meant playtime.

Miss Hudson's footsteps stomped up the stairs. They all froze, including Isla.

"I hope you've cleaned up whatever mess that came from that crash. And that better not have been my fine china!"

Irene leapt to her feet and grabbed the dog. "It's time for Isla's walk."

From his chair, Joe hissed at her. "Don't you leave me here!"

"It's just for an hour or so until Miss Hudson calms down." She grabbed a rogue pair of gloves from her table, then kissed Joe on the top of his head.

He went to grab for her but missed. "I took a bullet for you!"

"And I would take one for you, any day, any time. But I shall not endure Miss Hudson's wrath when I have such a lovely scapegoat."

"I'll remember this!" But his grin gave his true emotions away.

Irene stuck her hat on and flung open the door. "I'm sure you will, Joe! Ta-ta!"

She breezed past Miss Hudson, and soon Irene and Isla strolled down Baker Street, both happy as clams.

THE END

HOLMES & CO. WILL RETURN IN:

THE AMERICAN VISITORS

London is abuzz with the premiere of the film 'The Thief At Midnight'. The film's American stars, the beautiful Kathleen Carrington and the flirtatious Don Radcliffe, have come to Britain for the red carpet. However, they are met with vandalised posters and a message that clearly someone doesn't want Miss Carrington to leave London alive.

They request Irene and Joe specifically to search the hotel the actors are staying at – The Ritz, of course – and the theatre, for any signs of foul play. Just when Irene is about to rule this case a dud, a dead body turns up with the victim bearing a strange resemblance to Miss Kathleen Carrington herself. Irene, Joe, and DI Lestrade are swept up into the glitz and glamour of Hollywood as they attempt to keep the killer from striking again – all while trying to keep a low profile with the two biggest stars in the city.

About the Author

Allison Osborne lives in Ontario, Canada with her son, their West Highland terrier, and an overwhelming amount of vintage trinkets. She attended the University of Western Ontario for creative writing, and when her mind isn't wandering through 1940s England, she's busy dabbling in scriptwriting and other grand adventures.

Connect with Allison

Instagram: @allisonoauthor
Web: www.aosborneauthor.com